Little Bits of Sky

S. E. Durrant

Holiday House New York

Library of Congress Cataloging-in-Publication Data

Names: Durrant, S. E., author.
Title: Little bits of sky / S.E. Durrant.
Description: First American edition. | New York : Holiday House, 2017. |
"First published in the UK in 2016 by Nosy Crow Ltd, London." | Summary:
"Siblings Ira and Zac know the foster system inside and out, but it's only
when they are sent to Skilly House, a children's care home in London, that
their lives truly start to change"— Provided by publisher. | Summary: Ira
and her little brother, Zac, know the foster system well but their lives
start to change for the better when, in 1987, they go to Skilly House to live.
Identifiers: LCCN 2016056932 | ISBN 9780823438396 (hardcover)
Subjects: | CYAC: Orphanages—Fiction. | Orphans—Fiction. | Brothers
and sisters—Fiction. | Foster home care—Fiction. | Civil
disobedience—Fiction. | London (England)—History—20th century—Fiction.
| Great Britain—History—Elizabeth II, 1952—Fiction.
Classification: LCC PZ7.1.D875 Lit 2017 | DDC [Fic]—dc23 LC record
available at https://lccn.loc.gov/2016056932

For Duncan, Rosie, and Oliver

Today

This is the story of a time when my life turned upside down. Not that it was the right way up before, but for a while it felt like that moment when a clown juggles plates and they're all up in the air, and the only thing you can do is hold your breath and hope they don't come crashing to the ground.

I've put this story together from the diaries I kept when Zac and I were children. I wrote them because I felt we were almost invisible and I wanted to make sure our story was told, and also in the hope that life would get better for

the small unloved girl that was me, and my even smaller unloved brother. And if life didn't get better or at least more interesting, I was going to make it up—to put in witches and castles and rides in fast cars. But I didn't need to. Life got exciting all by itself.

My story starts at Skilly House. The garden there was the wildest place I had ever seen. There was a patch of grass big enough to run around in, and on all sides a tangle of scratchy bushes and shrubs, trailing ivy and a convolvulus that climbed the walls in summer, dotting the garden with flowers. There was a small overgrown pond covered with chicken wire, and there was the fallen tree.

I never felt entirely comfortable in Skilly House itself—it was too full of ghosts—but the garden was special. It was the first place I ever felt truly happy. I think Zac felt the same. Not that we wanted to go there, of course.

Skilly House
October 1987

My name's Miracle, but I don't tell anyone. It's embarrassing, especially for a care kid. Maybe my mum thought life would be wonderful and perfect when I was born, but it wasn't and it never has been. That's why everyone calls me Ira. My brother's called Zackery or Zac. Both names are okay, but Zac suits him better because he's always running. If you call him Zackery, he's gone before you get to the end of his name.

We didn't want to come to Skilly. We'd never been in a children's home, and anyway it wasn't fair we had to

move so suddenly. One minute we were eating dinner with Brenda and Alf, seeing how much ketchup we could balance on a chip, the next Anita was chasing us up to our room to pack our bags. I banged my suitcase all the way down the stairs, which is unusual for me. I normally keep my feelings to myself, being the oldest. Zac stood in the hall with that awful sad face he has when misery's wrapped itself around him so tight he looks like he's choking, and I know it will take ages to dig him out.

"Make sure you come and see us, won't you?" Brenda said as she hugged us good-bye.

And that made me feel really sad because I was nine years old and Zac was seven, and we already knew we'd never see them again. And she was the grown-up and she didn't know.

After that Zac made his mouth into a thin, flat line and that was that. There was no point trying to talk to him. We sat in Anita's car and watched the world go by. Our bit of the world, that is: South London.

At first Anita tried to chat. She told us about a James Bond film she saw. She said the actor was really handsome. She probably has his poster on her wall. But we didn't answer, so she gave up trying. I couldn't even think about James Bond. All I could think was, the car windows needed cleaning.

Anita's our social worker. She dyes her hair to match her lipstick. It's usually red, but we never know what kind of red it's going to be. Sometimes it's pink or orange. It takes our mind off things. Maybe that's why she does it. That day it was red like cherries. She looked like a film star stuck in the wrong film with two miserable kids in the back of her car, when really she should have been sky-diving or kissing a double agent.

It took us ages to get to Skilly. The traffic was all jammed up, and I thought the cars must look like ants from the sky. And I know ants are meant to know exactly what they're doing, but it made me wonder if they felt like we did inside. Lost.

When we finally stopped, we were on a street just like the one we came from. Nothing was any different. There were no fields or mountains or waterfalls or chimpanzees or kangaroos. There wasn't even a park. It was just a nor-mal London street with all the houses and flats squeezed in together like rotten teeth. If we hadn't been in the car for an hour, we'd have thought we just went around the corner.

As Anita parked the car, my heart started jumping around. It always does that just when I wish it would stay still, like if I want people to think I don't care what hap-pens when really I do. It's hard to look like you don't care what happens when your heart's doing somersaults.

Anita got out our suitcases and opened the gate to a crumbling old house. I had to pull Zac to make him come. He didn't want to move. He just wanted everything to stop there and then, like if the world could stop that would be good. When I pulled him he banged his head on the window. He didn't say anything, but I knew he hated me.

The house was tall and scruffy with white paint peeling off, like it had been painted a hundred years ago and nobody had bothered to tidy it up ever since. A man was tying a rosebush to the wall. He was trying to stop the roses trailing on the ground. They were small and red and their petals were falling off, but he still wanted to tie them up. I expect they looked nice in summer.

Anita said, "Hello," and the man turned around.

He was wearing an old leather jacket and his hair was full of ringlets, not shiny like a princess but all tangled and sticking out. He smiled when he saw us, and his face filled with creases. I didn't want to like him, but I couldn't help it.

"I think the wind's going to blow up a bit," he said.

He waved a bit of string.

He shook Anita's hand, and then he shook ours. I acted like I always shake hands, but really it was the first time it ever happened. Zac's hand went all floppy like when he

pretends he's ill. People don't normally shake hands with care kids. Sometimes they don't even look at us.

"I'm Silas," the man said. "Welcome to Skilly."

He's the only Silas I've ever met. He's probably the only one in London. People don't call their kids Silas anymore. It's an olden-days name.

We walked to the front door, and he rang the bell. There was a sign on the wall that said SKILLY HOUSE 1887, which means it was built a hundred years ago, which is a century. I thought of all the kids who must have stood on the doorstep before us, wondering what would happen next. Maybe their mum had been run over by a horse and carriage or their dad had gotten stuck up a chimney, or maybe they just ran out of luck. I turned my face to stone so whoever opened the door wouldn't see how I felt inside. Zac was taking lots of breaths like he was tired out. Only he wasn't tired out. He was scared.

But the woman who opened the door wasn't scary at all. She was beautiful. She was smiling and smiling, like she'd been looking forward to seeing us all day, and finally we'd come.

"Children!" she said. "Come in, come in. We've been waiting for you."

She put out her arms and wrapped them around us. It felt so nice. She had yellow beads on the ends of her

dreadlocks, and they bounced like bees. I wanted to hold one, but I didn't. I just touched one really gently so she wouldn't notice. It felt lucky.

Silas said, "This is Hortense. She'll settle you in."

Then he went back to his rosebush.

We went inside with Hortense and stood in the hall. It was dark and the stairs went up and up, and I tried to imagine them going all the way up to the sky and at the top there'd be a big burst of light. Then I had a feeling someone was watching us, and when I turned around I saw a woman standing in a doorway. I thought she was a ghost at first. A shiver went right down my spine. She was very thin and she was standing as still as a skeleton and she was staring at me and Zac like she wished we'd never arrived. Like if she could wind back time, she'd make us walk right back out of the door and lock it behind us.

Hortense said, "Meet Mrs. Clanks, manager of Skilly," and the woman came over.

She walked really straight like a soldier and her shoes went *tap-tap* on the floor, so I knew she was real. Ghosts don't make noises. It takes all their effort just to be here at all. That's why you don't see them much.

She was old and her hair was tied back, and she had a frown between her eyes that looked like it had been there forever. Like she might have been the first baby ever to

be born with a frown. She was wearing boring grown-up clothes, except for one thing: she had a pink shiny ribbon in her hair. I wondered if someone had put it there and she didn't know yet. But it didn't make me want to laugh. It made me embarrassed.

She shook Anita's hand and said, "Good afternoon."

Then she smiled at me and Zac. Only it wasn't the kind of smile that makes you glad to be there. It was the kind of smile you give someone when you wish they lived hundreds of miles away, like in Australia.

"Hortense will show you your room," she said.

She said it just like that. Not "Hello" or "How was your journey?" She said it like a plumber had come to fix a leak, and she had to tell them where the pipes were. And they better get on with it before everything flooded. Not like some kids had come to their new home where they might have to stay forever.

I wanted to shout that we weren't staying. I had to grit my teeth to stop it coming out. I wanted to shout that we hated it here already, and we were going back to Brenda and Alf. But I couldn't. Zac would be upset, and anyway it never works. Even if the cutest little kid makes a fuss, nothing changes. Not if they're a care kid.

Anita usually smiles when she leaves us because smiles spread. If one person smiles, that makes the next person

smile and it goes on and on. You can cheer up a whole crowd of people that way. It's like magic. But that day she couldn't smile. Her face just wouldn't make the right shape. She knelt down in front of me and Zac and gave us a kiss.

"Off you go," she said. "I'll see you soon."

She still looked like a film star, only now she was in a war film watching her children be evacuated to the country, and she was being brave. She left cherry lipstick on Zac's cheek, then she wiped it away.

We followed Hortense up the stairs. I pretended she was an angel taking us to heaven, but I couldn't do it for long. Kids were peering at us through the banisters and sticking out their tongues. A tall boy threw a ball of paper at my shoulder. I pretended I hadn't noticed, but I could hear him sniggering.

The stair carpet was so old you could see threads where the soft bits had worn away. It might have been nice once because it still had flower patterns, but now they were muddy like at the bottom of a pond. Every step creaked, and the creaks were all in different places. Some were in the middle of the step and some were on the edges and some steps seemed fine, but when you took your foot off they gave a little squeak. You could never go up or down those steps quietly; you'd have to learn where the creaks were.

There were drawings on the walls and writing that had

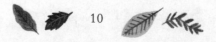

been smudged out, maybe because it said someone loved someone else and they changed their mind, or maybe because it said something horrible.

And there was dust on every step. I had to try really hard not to think about it because dust comes from dead skin, so it must have come from the children who walked up the stairs before us. Maybe even from children who are dead. I just concentrated on counting the steps. I always do that in new places. I always count the steps going up so I know how many I have to go down. It's one of my habits. From the hall up to our room is forty-seven steps.

Our bedroom is right at the top of the house. You can't go any farther. It's nice like that. No one walks past. When we got there Hortense said, "Best room in the house," and opened the door like we'd just arrived on holiday or something, not in a children's home.

But actually it's okay. It's got a sloping roof on one side and a window on the other, and from the window you can see the garden. There were two beds with duvets and bobbly blankets, and there was a sink with yellow stains going from the taps to the plughole. There was a wardrobe and some drawers and a table, and there was tape stuck to the walls where kids had taken off their posters. There was a rug on the floor that was so old the color had faded away, and under the rug were floorboards.

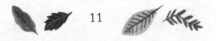

11

Hortense put her head to one side and looked at us like a heron searching for fish in a pond.

"It'll feel very different when you've settled in," she said.

Then she opened the window and a breeze came into the room, and it felt lovely. I looked out and saw a bird fly into a tree.

"Now," Hortense said, "come and see the garden."

The garden at Skilly is amazing. It's huge and raggedy and full of hiding places, and even though there are buildings all around, it feels like it's on its own. There was a shed and a pond with chicken wire over the top, and there was a huge tree in the middle. When the sun came through the leaves, it made patches of light on the grass.

We had the garden all to ourselves that afternoon. We didn't know then, but that's what they do with new kids. They let them play in the garden on their own. At first Zac wouldn't let go of my hand, but then he found a stick and started hitting the tree. Bits of bark were flying off. I didn't say anything. I just walked away. Then I spun around and around until I was so dizzy I had to lie down, and as I lay there I let my head fill up with the blue sky, and then I didn't want to shout anymore. That's the thing about the sky. No matter how bad things are, you can always look up at the sky, and then you feel better.

Afterward we had tea in the kitchen with the other kids. They hardly even looked at us. I pretended not to look at them either, but really I kept taking glances. They all did different things with their food. It showed their personalities. Some ate really quickly and wanted more, some only ate the best bits; some just pushed their food around their plate and didn't eat at all. Some kids made a mess, and some were really tidy and put their knives and forks together when they finished like they were in a restaurant and the waiter would come and take their plates. The boy who threw the paper at me didn't even chew. He gulped his food down like it was melted ice cream even though it was shepherd's pie. When Hortense wasn't looking, he put some mashed potato on his fork and flicked it at me. It landed in the middle of my plate. I didn't eat after that. It put me off.

As soon as we could get away, we ran up to our room and looked out at the garden. It was nice to be so high up. It's like being invisible. It was dark and windy outside, and the tree was shaking. Two pigeons were sitting in the branches, but they didn't mind. They just rocked from side to side. They were used to it. Silas was carrying some tools into the shed, and his hair was blowing in his eyes.

Then we got into our beds and just sat there for ages. I didn't read or draw or anything. I wanted to be paying attention for when Zac spoke.

At last he said, "Why are the walls so high?"

It was the first thing he said since we left Brenda and Alf's.

"It's an old house," I said. "That's how they made them."

"Were people taller then?" he said.

"No," I said. "I think they were smaller."

He looked annoyed.

"Why then?" he said.

"I don't know."

"Can I get in with you?" he said.

I nodded.

He ran to my bed and curled up beside me. People like Zac because when he's not sad or angry, he's funny. He makes up games and he can run really fast, and he likes to chase people or be chased and to run down the street ringing doorbells. And kids like that even if grown-ups don't. Especially old ladies don't.

But Zac doesn't like other people. Not really. He doesn't trust them. The only person he trusts is me, so I can never let him down. He's my responsibility.

"What will it be like here?" he said.

"It'll be okay."

We could hear people talking downstairs.

"Do you think there are ghosts?"

I shook my head, but really I was wondering too. I

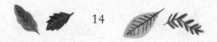

wasn't worried about the kind you can see through, or the kind that look like sheets. I was worried about all the children who lived in Skilly before us and all the clues they left behind, like the scribbles on the walls, and all the sad eyes that must have looked out of the windows and wished they were somewhere else.

"No," I said. "There's no such thing as ghosts."

Zac's mouth was wobbling.

"Shall I tell you a story?" I said.

"The special one?"

"If you want."

He nodded.

I always make up stories for Zac. Usually he kills a monster and rescues the villagers or the schoolchildren or the sailors who are drowning because a sea monster sank their boat. But the special story is different because I don't know if I made it up or not.

Zac always says things like, "What was Mum like? Did she cuddle me?" And he doesn't want me to say I don't know, so I have to give him an answer. And that's how we got our story.

"Mum was holding you," I said. "You were really tiny and you were holding her finger like you'd never let go, and she was kissing you and her hair was curly like ours, and she thought we'd be happy forever."

I stroked his hair and his eyes flopped shut and then he was asleep. That's what he's like. All he has to do is close his eyes.

I couldn't get to sleep. I kept thinking about all the people we'd lived with before we came to Skilly. I always knew we wouldn't stay with Brenda and Alf for long. They were old, and Alf kept losing things. He needed Brenda to look after him, not us. Before them there was Petra, who got a job working night shifts so she couldn't look after us anymore, and there was Alara, who kept telling us we wouldn't be there for Christmas (and we weren't). There were the Grimbles, who said they'd keep us forever, but then their new baby arrived. And there was Adam, who didn't have enough chairs for everyone to sit down at the same time. And then there were all the short stays with people we called Nan or Auntie but who weren't relatives at all, and the woman who was mean to us so Anita had to take us away.

I used to tell Zac we were like gypsies—always traveling to exciting places—but I stopped saying it because it didn't make moving exciting. It made it worse. But that night I pretended there was a horse sleeping outside and an old-fashioned caravan with flowers painted on it, and in the morning we'd go on an adventure. We'd go down a long road with grass on both sides and trees blowing in the wind, and there'd be hills in the distance, and me and

Zac would be holding the reins and singing. And then I realized I didn't know if horses sleep standing up or lying down and I was trying to work it out, and I think that's when I fell asleep.

The Storm

At first I thought I was having a nightmare. I was bumping all the way down the stairs. The banging was really loud, and I was trying to count the steps and thinking it's going to really hurt when I got to the bottom. But when I woke up, I could still hear banging. Zac was holding on to me really tight and digging his fingers into my arm. His eyes were squeezed shut.

"Ghosts!" he whispered.

But I knew it wasn't ghosts. I could hear the wind howling outside. I jumped out of bed and ran to the window. It was the middle of the night, and a storm was crashing through the garden. It was pulling up bushes and ripping pieces of wood off the shed and throwing them into the air. The tree was rocking from side to side, and all the time the wind was wailing. It was like when a kid has the worst tantrum ever, and you know you won't be able to calm them down. You just have to wait for it to be over and hope they don't break too much.

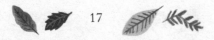

"Zac!" I called. "Look!"

Zac got to the window just as the tree blew over. It was amazing! The wind was pushing it so hard, it went diagonal, and then suddenly it couldn't get up again and crashed to the ground. As it fell it howled like it was a dying animal, and its roots came up and they were being blown by the wind, so it looked like the tree was still alive. Like an antelope being eaten by lions. Only it wasn't alive. It was dead.

At first me and Zac could hardly breathe. Then we started laughing like we were on a ride at the fair. We felt sick, but it was brilliant. We could hear people running around downstairs, but we didn't go down. We just sat on my bed and listened to the storm, and I crossed my fingers and hoped the house wouldn't blow over.

Seeing the tree blow down was one of the best things I ever saw. I know it shouldn't be, but it was.

The storm was gone by the next morning. I don't know if it went somewhere else, but it wasn't in London. We couldn't wait to see what had happened. All the Skilly kids ran out into the street. We didn't even have breakfast. Another tree had blown down right across the road and landed on a car. There was a dent in the roof, and the windscreen was smashed into tiny pieces. I don't think you could ever fix it.

Bins were blown over too, and rubbish had gone everywhere. There was a banana skin stuck in the branches of the tree and some plastic bottles and lots of wrappers. An old man wearing a bathrobe was sweeping glass off his path, and two women were trying to get a bike off some railings. It was twisted on so it looked like a cartoon, and there was a crisp packet stuck in the wheel. The women were half laughing and half annoyed. Because even though the storm was amazing, the bike was ruined.

Silas's rosebush had completely disappeared. Even the string was gone. It probably went miles. It might even have landed in someone else's garden, and in summer people would wonder where the red roses came from, because maybe they only planted white. Silas wasn't annoyed, though. He was laughing.

"I didn't think it was going to be *this* windy," he said. "Go down in history, it will."

And it really will, because it was the biggest storm for three hundred years. That means even before Skilly was built and when women wore long dresses and couldn't vote or go to school. And there were no cars or TV and there was no electricity, and people played the piano in the dark and the whole family would sing along. Me and Zac might be in history books too, because we saw what happened.

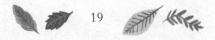

On the news it showed what else the storm had done. There was a house with its roof blown right off. You could see into the bedroom. You could even see what kind of wallpaper the people had and what books they were reading.

The wind blew lorries over too. It just picked them up and threw them on to their sides, and they were lying across the motorway like elephants that poachers had killed to take the tusks. And the wind threw trailers into the sea so all the pots and pans were floating around.

We Skilly kids were really excited. We already knew everything could be turned upside down at any moment, and now everyone else could see it too. We ran into the back garden and climbed onto the tree and just kept staring at it because we couldn't believe it was lying on the ground when it used to be up in the sky. We kept running along the trunk and jumping off the roots, and we did it over and over, and every time felt just as amazing as the first time.

Silas cut the branches off the tree, and we gathered them up and put them in a pile with the wood from the shed. And as the leaves and twigs crunched under my feet, I had to stop and take a deep breath because I realized I was happy and I was so surprised.

"We'll have a great fire with this lot," Silas said.

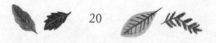

And we did. On Bonfire Night we stood in the garden and ate hot potatoes and watched the flames flickering in the big hole where the tree used to be.

The tree's been lying in the garden ever since. Silas cut steps into it so the little kids can get onto the top. The bark's crumbling and covered in moss and kids have written their names on it. I scratched *Ira and Zac were here 10/16/87* into one of the steps, because we saw the tree fall and that makes us part of its history, and also because it was our first whole day at Skilly. The kids here call the tree the ship or the raft, and we run along the top of it or hide behind it and ambush each other. And when the garden's quiet I lean against it and draw, or just shut my eyes and listen, because when no one's outside the garden sort of hums.

Photo of a Dog
March 1989

It's been nearly a year and a half since me and Zac came to Skilly. All the kids who were here when we first came have gone, apart from the boy who flicked mashed potatoes at me. The others have been fostered or adopted or gone home and new kids have come instead, but Jimmy's still here. He goes away, then he comes back, then he goes away again. Nothing works out for him. Maybe it's because he's so tall. Maybe it's even worse than having curly hair like me and Zac. But I don't think so. I think

it's because he's angry. Even when he's happy, he's angry. Even when he's laughing and telling jokes, you can tell he's a little bit angry underneath.

I never know what he's going to do next and he makes me nervous, but he's still one of my favorites because he's full of life. He doesn't like life very much, but it bursts out of him anyway. He can't help it. It's like he's got bouncy shoes.

He does little skips and jumps when he walks, and if his favorite song comes on the radio, he dances. He knows all the words and moves. He looks like a pop star. Sometimes Hortense joins in too. She can't help it either, and then they're both dancing and laughing. That's the thing about Jimmy. Even though he's angry he makes people happy.

But apart from Jimmy, me and Zac have been here longest. Hortense says that means we're old hands. We're supposed to show new kids what to do, but usually they don't want anything to do with us. Being old hands isn't something to be proud of. It's something to be ashamed of.

When new kids come to Skilly, they're either loud and angry or secretive and quiet. The angry kids tell everyone about their lives, what their families are like and where they've come from. They say they're not staying, and they try to fight other kids because they don't want to fit in. They tell lies too. One kid said his mum was a

millionaire, and another said her dad was a TV chef. But I'm sure they were lying, because rich kids like that don't go into care. Someone always wants them.

The quiet kids are the opposite. They don't say anything. They keep their secrets to themselves so no one can take them away. Really, they want to be invisible. Usually the angry kids have to fight each other because the quiet kids don't want to.

People probably think me and Zac are the secretive kind, but we're not really. It's just that we don't have anything to tell. We don't have parents, and there's nothing to show we ever did have parents. We've got a Memory Book full of photos and birthday cards, but everything in the book comes from being in care.

Except one photo.

There's one photo of us that was taken somewhere else. If you look at it quickly it looks like a photo of a dog—a big black hairy dog jumping towards the camera, his tongue poking over his lips. The dog takes up nearly all the picture, and when people see it for the first time they say, "Oh look, a photo of a dog."

But if you look closely, you can see the dog's jumping out of an armchair and me and Zac are sitting on each side. We're almost squashed out of the picture, but not quite. Zac's a baby and he's propped up with a cushion

and he looks surprised, and I'm on the other side, a bit blurred, as if I jumped when the dog jumped. I'm nearly two years old. We know it's us because the photo has *Miracle and Zackery, July 1980* written on the back in someone's writing. I don't know whose, and I don't know where the chair was, and I don't know who the dog was. And that's it. It's hard to get any information from a picture like that. I sometimes wonder what happened to the dog, but I expect it's dead by now.

And apart from that photo, there's nothing to show we ever had a family. Except we look the same—two curly-haired kids. Same but different.

Anita says we had a mum once, but she couldn't look after us any more. It's what people say to care kids. It doesn't really mean anything. It's like saying it's cold outside when really it could be stormy or wet or snowy or icy and you haven't got a window so you can't check. All you know is you'd better put your coat on.

I said, "Can't she come to visit?" but Anita said, "We don't know where she is."

Then she looked so sad, I wished I hadn't asked. She looked like she'd come for a party and arrived on the wrong day.

I don't think me and Zac will ever get a family. This is why, in no particular order:

We're not little anymore.
Every time someone doesn't want us, it shows a little bit.
We want to stay together.

Anita keeps trying to find us a family. She doesn't give up. When we came to Skilly, she advertised us in the paper next to the holiday cottages so people would see us if they were looking for somewhere nice to stay. They might even think of us if there was a spare room, so as not to waste it. A photographer hung a sheet in the hall and Hortense threw a ball in the air, and me and Zac sat in front of the sheet and looked at the ball and smiled. We've got the photo in our Memory Book and we saw the advert in the paper. It said:

Sister and brother, aged nine and seven, need a family. Ira loves reading and drawing; Zac loves being outdoors and takes a while to settle.

But the trouble with photos is people can see what you look like. There's nothing you can do about it. I think people would like us better if they got to know us first instead of looking at a photo. We tried to look sweet, but nobody came. I curled my fingers into my palm to hide my chewed nails, but nobody came.

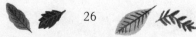

And now I'm ten and a half and Zac's nine, and Anita said as we get older it'll be harder to find us a family. I said, "Well, no one wanted us anyway." She said maybe the right people don't know about us yet. But I think there are too many people for the right ones to find us. There are millions of people just in London, so the chances of finding the right two must be really tiny. By the time they find us we will be grown up, and it'll be too late. And that would be even worse than not finding us at all.

I try not to think about my dream home too much because it makes me sad, but I'm going to write it down just this one time. Because writing things down makes them real, and things don't happen if they're not real. You have to tell someone, even if it's just a diary.

My dream home will have a front door just for me and Zac and our mum and dad, and a key we hang in the hall. There'll be wallpaper and flowers and not too many rooms. There'll be stairs that don't creak, and I'll have my own bedroom with a desk and drawers for my art materials. There'll be a goal in the garden for Zac, and at the end of the road there'll be a sweetshop with old-fashioned jars and flying saucers and sherbet lemons.

I haven't imagined my mum and dad, but if they're not beautiful or handsome or clever or rich it won't matter as long as they're nice.

Skilly's nothing like my dream home, but it's okay. Even

though me and Zac share a room, it's okay. Zac put up his Arsenal poster because that's his favorite team. He knows the names of all the players. I put up my *Matilda* poster because *Matilda*'s my favorite book. It's about a girl who's got horrible parents, but it doesn't matter because she can make things happen just by thinking. I've tried to do that myself, thinking really hard, but it doesn't work. It feels like it should, but it doesn't. My poster's a drawing of Matilda thinking really hard, but you can't tell what she's thinking and you can't see what she's changing. Sometimes I imagine she's thinking about me and Zac and she's going to make our life much, much better.

But the problem with the posters is that Zac's Arsenal poster is above his bed so I have to look at it, and my *Matilda* poster's above my bed so Zac has to look at it. We tried it the other way around but it didn't feel right— it's one of those problems people don't realize if they don't share a room.

The very best thing about our room is the only thing above it is the sky. When I wake up in the morning, I think about the birds flying over me, and when Zac can't sleep I tell him there's an owl sitting on the roof and the owl knows all the secrets of the world. And that makes him feel safe.

My favorite hobby is drawing. I draw flowers and

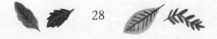

28

nature and people, and sometimes I do sketches called caricatures. I started doing caricatures when I was trying to draw Zac; I couldn't get him right, so I gave him a long nose and he looked really funny. I like drawing people this way—the way I see them instead of the way they actually are.

I've done lots of pictures of Skilly kids. I've drawn the boy with the knobbly knees who stayed for a week, and the kid who gelled his hair into a spike, and the girl with rings in her nose. I've drawn the short kids, the fat kids, the tall ones and the thin ones. Sometimes I put them in a line with the really tall ones next to the really small ones, and sometimes I make up kids who've never been here.

I've also drawn Silas with his hair tangled like a lion and Hortense with wings because she's like an angel, and Mrs. Clanks as a skeleton. I've drawn Zac riding a dinosaur and as a pirate and as a strongman at the circus. I've even drawn him as a bouncy ball, because that's what he's like. He always bounces back.

The only people I don't draw are the children who lived here before us. I try not to think about them because they must be old now or dead. If I see reminders like scribbles on the wall, I think about something else.

But there's one girl I can't help thinking about. She

scratched her name into our windowsill, so every time I look at the garden I think of her. It says *Glenda Hyacinth, 1947*, which is forty-two years ago. She must have stood at the window too, and that means she lived in our room and she's probably dead now and that makes her a ghost. And then I remember that I scratched me and Zac into the fallen tree, and we'll be ghosts one day too. And that makes me feel horrible.

But mostly Skilly's okay. And when I feel sorry for myself, I talk to Silas. He tells me one day things will be different.

Silas

Silas is the best person ever. He's not like a grown-up. He doesn't mind mess, he doesn't get angry and he can fix things. He always smells of fresh air. It's like he's got the outdoors wrapped round him. If someone made that smell into perfume, they'd be rich. It could go in a little green bottle with a daisy lid. Everyone would want to buy some.

Silas is full of life like Jimmy, but he doesn't have bouncy shoes. Life comes out of him in a different way, like leaves in a breeze. He's never still for one minute. He can't help it. Sometimes he has tea with us in the kitchen,

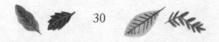

and even though he's sitting at the table, he's rocking and his fingers are moving and his face is smiling and laughing and frowning all at the same time. It's because his head's full of memories.

He's been all over the world and done loads of things. We get him to tell us his stories over and over again. Sometimes he says, "Haven't I told you that already?" but we always say no, because Skilly kids want to know his stories by heart so we can pretend we were there ourselves.

When he was younger he lived in Australia. He rode horses and looked after cattle. It's called being a rancher. If you could dig a hole right down through the pavement and keep digging, you'd end up in his ranch. Only there's fire in the middle of the world, so you can't go through. You have to go around. When it's daytime in Australia it's night here, so when everyone in London was sleeping Silas was riding his horse, and when everyone in London was having breakfast he was looking at the stars. It sounds confusing, but it isn't, because the sun tells you when it's time to get up or go to bed.

He's been in the rain forest too. He says if you stand really still and listen, you can hear insects running over the leaves and little drops of water falling. He's also been to India and he's seen cows sit in the middle of the road

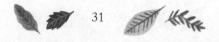

and not move, even though cars are hooting at them and there's a traffic jam. The cows even go to sleep there. They don't mind. And he's seen spices so bright they made his eyes hurt.

One time he was camping in a forest, and when he woke up there was a python in his sleeping bag. Pythons can swallow a crocodile whole, so it could easily have eaten Silas. He had to lie really still until the snake woke up and slithered out. He lay there all day, just keeping calm and hoping the python wasn't hungry. You have to be very brave not to move if a python's in your bed. Me and Zac tried pretending, and we couldn't do it. And that's without a real python. If we had been there, we'd have been eaten.

"I dreamed of that snake," Silas said. "I dreamed it was there and I knew not to stretch out my legs, and that dream saved my life. Sixth sense, I call it."

We don't learn about sixth sense at school. We just learn the five main ones: hearing, smell, sight, touch and taste. My teacher said to imagine using them when someone's cooking dinner, but it's more fun to imagine them when someone's burning dinner. You hear hissing, you smell burning, you see the burned pan, you touch the hot handle and you taste the burned food. Then you spit it out.

But sixth sense is different. It's sort of invisible. I think it's like knowing someone's burned the dinner even though you're not back from school yet. Silas says we'll recognize it when we need it. He says if you trust it, it can get you out of trouble.

But the best thing about Silas is he's a care kid like us, so he understands how we feel. All he knows about his family is his dad was named Bernard and his mum was named Hilda. He doesn't even know why they named him Silas. He was born in London in the war, and when he was a baby a bomb landed on his house and killed his mum and dad. They just couldn't get out quick enough. Hilda was probably trying to get him into his little jumper and Bernard was probably getting him some milk.

"I was pulled out of the rubble," he said, "and passed from one pair of hands to the next. Just like you lot."

He went to live on a farm away from the bombs, and when the war finished he didn't have anywhere to go, so he stayed in the countryside and got moved from one place to the next.

"I used to think I could be picked up and carried anywhere," he said, "but I learned something you lot should understand. They can take you anywhere they like, but they can't choose where this goes."

And he banged his hand on his chest where his heart

must be. I know what he meant. If you don't have a family, you have to hold on extra tight to what's inside. I hold on to my heart really tight. Zac holds his even tighter.

Skilly Kids

Apart from me, Zac, and Jimmy, there's six other kids at Skilly. This is them—not in any special order, just how they come into my head.

Sophia's the oldest. She's fourteen. She's kind and quiet and doesn't say anything about herself. She's like me and Zac in that way. She writes poems on a little typewriter, and sometimes you can hear her typing in her room. But then she hides her poems so you can never read them. She braids her hair and wears bright shirts, which is funny because she doesn't really like to be noticed, and if you wear bright shirts people notice you. She looks like a pop star, but I've never heard her sing.

Ashani's the youngest. She's eight. She wishes she was a boy because she wants to be a footballer when she grows up and she wants to play at Wembley. She supports Crystal Palace, and when she talks about football she says things like, "We only lost because the ref was rubbish and our striker was injured." She makes it sound like Crystal Palace played best even if they didn't win.

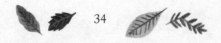

She's got a Crystal Palace shirt, but it's too big for her. It's probably big enough for Jimmy. Hortense sewed it up, but the shoulders still come to her elbows.

Ashani's everyone's favorite. She makes funny faces and she laughs a lot and she's easy to make happy. If I was going to adopt someone, I'd adopt Ashani. Then I'd buy her a Crystal Palace shirt that fits and take her to a real live football match so she didn't have to watch it on TV. And I'd buy her chips afterward, and Coke.

Esther's nine. She loves yellow. She doesn't feel like herself if she's not wearing it. She feels like someone she doesn't like. She gets upset if her clothes get messy, and when she came to Skilly she was angry because she wants to live somewhere pretty. She's the same age as Zac, but he doesn't like her. Sometimes she plays dressing up and wants him to be her husband. But Zac doesn't want to play families. He wants to play knights and soldiers. And he doesn't want to rescue a princess either.

Miles is thirteen like Jimmy, but he's small so you can't tell. When he first came, Jimmy wanted to fight Miles but Miles just walked away. He's got tiny hands, and he spends ages in his room making things with sticks or taking things apart and putting them back together. Hortense gives him matches when she's used them, so they can't catch fire, and he makes stick men or houses out of

them. One time Silas made holes in chestnuts, and Miles put matches through the holes so they were like wheels on little cars, and we had races with them. They didn't last long, though. They kept breaking.

Milap and Harit are ten and nine, and they're brothers. Milap is really good at magic. He can make little red balls disappear and then appear somewhere else. He can do card tricks too, and he knows what your card is even though he can't see it. Harit likes animals, especially extinct ones. He's like Zac because he knows all the names of dinosaurs. His favorite is *Triceratops*, which is the one with three horns. Zac likes *Tyrannosaurus rex* best.

But Milap and Harit are always waiting to leave Skilly. You can feel it. Even if you're talking to them, it's like a bit of them isn't listening properly in case the doorbell rings and it's their mum come to get them. Their mum's in the hospital because she got worried and her brain needs a rest, and their dad couldn't look after them because he got sad thinking about their mum. It's called mental illness. You can't see it like a broken leg, but it's just as bad. Maybe worse. When their mum gets better they're all going to get back together again, because then their dad will be happier too. Then they can go home.

Easter

We all got Easter eggs today with our names written on them in squiggly chocolate writing. Ashani said she saw Mrs. Clanks taking them out of a bag and putting them on the kitchen table, but I don't think so. I think Mrs. Clanks was taking them off the kitchen table and putting them in a bag. That's what she's like. She doesn't want us to have fun. It was lucky Ashani walked in.

After breakfast Silas hid the eggs in the garden, and we had an egg hunt. Jimmy found his first. I found Milap's, Milap found Esther's, Esther found Sophia's and Sophia found mine, so we all swapped. It's the first time I ever saw "Ira" written in chocolate. It looked so nice. If it was always written in chocolate, I'd like it much better.

We all found our eggs really quickly, apart from Zac. Jimmy had nearly eaten his and Ashani kept getting us to hide hers again, but Zac hadn't even found his for the first time yet. He was beginning to get upset. Silas looked worried because he hid eight eggs and he couldn't remember where they all were.

Esther said, "You can have mine if you like," but Zac said, "No thanks, it's got *Esther* on it!"

I was thinking how quickly things get spoiled when

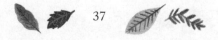

Harit said, "Look!" and there was Zac's egg hidden behind the ivy, high up on the wall. Silas was surprised because he'd hidden them all low down, so I think Jimmy moved it. Anyway it was all okay.

Eating an egg with your name on it is one of the nicest things in the world. But it does have to be your own name.

My Perfect Day
April 1989

There's daffodils and daisies in the garden now. It shows summer's coming. I tried to draw them today, but I couldn't even make them look like flowers, so I put little legs on them and made them into insects. They looked funny crawling across the page.

Zac and Harit were chasing each other with bows and arrows but I didn't mind as long as they kept away from me. I was sitting in a patch of sun, and it was really warm on my back. Silas was in his garden next door.

Silas lives in the bungalow next to Skilly. We're not allowed in his garden, but if we see him we talk to him over the fence. Unless Mrs. Clanks sees us, because then she comes out and tells us off. She says things like, "Isn't Silas allowed some time to himself?" And all the time she's flapping her hands to keep insects away. She doesn't like nature. She's an indoors sort of person. Zac says he's going to put a spider down her back one day, but I know he won't. She's too scary. It's just one of his dreams, like fighting dinosaurs. I don't think even Jimmy would do it.

But Silas likes talking to us. He says things like, "How's it going?" or "What you up to?" One time he showed us a beetle. It had a green and blue shield on its back that looked like a shell. It's called a shield bug. The shield's meant to protect it, but it hadn't worked because the beetle was dead when Silas found it. Now Zac's got it. He put it on our windowsill, next to Glenda Hyacinth's name. I moved it along in case she didn't like insects, but she might not mind. It's quite pretty.

Silas is always finding things. That's why his garden's full of junk. He says it'll come in handy one day, but I don't know how. He's got an old table and piles of wood and pots of paint and a broken chair and a cage with a wheel but no hamster in it. Usually he's got a pint mug of tea, which is a whole teapot full.

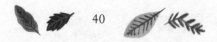

One time at school everyone had to say what their perfect day would be and I couldn't even imagine because I've never done anything perfect. My heart was beating so loud, I thought the whole class would hear. Other kids were saying things like going to Disneyland or camping next to a stream, but when my turn came I had to say I didn't know. It was embarrassing. But actually, I think my perfect day is drawing in the garden with the sun shining and Zac playing and Silas in his garden too. So I think today was my perfect day.

When I finished drawing I went to talk to Silas over the fence. He was hammering a nail into some wood.

"What are you making?" I said.

"I'll show you."

He lifted up a stick with a bit of board nailed to it. It looked like a giant lollipop.

"Is it a placard?" I said.

He nodded.

"It's just to tell people what I think."

Me and Zac see placards every day on the way to school. People stand outside the library with them, even if it's pouring with rain. I think they must take sandwiches, because they're still there when we're walking home. They've usually got No Poll Tax or Can't Pay, Won't Pay written on their placards, but they don't look too fed up.

"Are you going to stand outside the library?" I said.

"No," Silas said. "I'm going on a march."

"About the poll tax?"

He nodded.

"With other people?"

He laughed. "I hope so."

Hortense says the poll tax isn't for kids to worry about. It's a grown-up thing. She says it's money grown-ups have to pay, but lots of people are worried because it costs too much. That's why they have placards. So they can tell everyone it's a bad idea. She says history's full of people holding placards.

I've seen lots of placards. Sometimes they say Only God Can Save You, and sometimes they say Charlie's Jerk Chicken 99p. It all depends.

But I think life would be more straightforward if everyone had a placard, because then you don't have to say what you think out loud so you don't have to be rude. It's like shouting without making a noise. You could maybe even stop a war that way.

"I wish I had a placard," I said.

Silas said, "What would you write on it?"

"I'd write 'Leave Me Alone' for when kids keep pestering me."

He laughed. "Mine would say 'Any Chance of a Cup of Tea?'"

After that I kept thinking of different things to write.

Zac's placard would say ARE YOU MY MUM? Because every time he sees a woman who looks like us, he thinks she's our mum. If he had a placard, he could stand in the street and people could come up and say yes or no, or they could just walk past but at least he wouldn't have to keep asking me. I expect most would walk past. Maybe all.

Esther's would say HAVE YOU GOT THAT IN YELLOW? Milap and Harit's would say WAS THAT THE DOORBELL? Ashani's would say CRYSTAL PALACE FOREVER or THAT WAS A FOUL or THE BOYS WERE UNLUCKY.

I'd have different placards for different occasions. I'd have the one saying LEAVE ME ALONE for if I was reading or drawing. I'd lean it against my chair so I could hold on to my book. And I'd have one for when people are being horrible or telling me off. I'd hold it up in front of Mrs. Clanks or my teacher or Skilly kids when they're making me feel bad. It would say STOP NOW! And I'd have another one for when Zac's embarrassing me, like when he rings people's doorbells and runs away. It would say THAT BOY IS NOT MY BROTHER.

My Favorite People

These are my favorite people. There aren't many. If I die and there's a funeral, not many people will come because I don't know many people. If I had a family, I'd have cousins and aunts and grandparents, but I've only got Zac. I've written a list just in case. Zac's at the top, even though he's annoying sometimes.

Silas and Hortense are next. Silas because he's the best person in the world, and Hortense because sometimes she puts her arm around me and gives me a kiss and I don't even know why, and apart from Anita she's the only person who's kissed me for years and years. Also, she goes to church to say prayers and sing hymns, which makes her really good. I hope she says prayers for me and Zac because if I was God, Hortense is exactly the sort of person I'd listen to because she's like an angel.

Anita's on the list as well; she's always looking out for us, and even though she must be fed up of looking out for two kids nobody wants, she doesn't show it. She just keeps on trying to cheer us up and surprising us with her hair.

The Skilly kids are on my list too. I put Jimmy and Ashani at the top because they're my favorites. All the others are on the same line because I can't choose between them. I like them all the same.

I also put Amanda and Kaleigh from my class on the list, but I put them at the bottom. Because I don't always know if they're going to be nice, and I'm not even sure if I like them. I put them at the bottom so I can tear them off or fold the paper over if I change my mind.

Mrs. Clanks isn't on my list because she makes me feel bad. At first I thought she was a ghost, but now I know she's just a horrible living person. I hope she never becomes a ghost because if she does, Skilly will be haunted forever, and nobody will want to come in because all the kids would die of fright. Even as a living person, she spoils things. She's always trying to catch kids doing something wrong, and she's always thinking things and you can't tell what they are, except they're not very nice.

Jimmy said she locked a boy in a cupboard once and left him there, and he died. He told Zac, and Zac told me. Zac's eyes were really wide like he was scared and excited. Like when the tree blew down.

He said, "And when the boy died he became a skeleton, and someone opened the cupboard and the skeleton fell out, and no one knew who he was or even if it was a boy or a girl because you can't tell with skeletons."

I said, "Don't be stupid, Zac; she couldn't do that. Someone would find out."

But Zac said, "It's true. Jimmy says so, and he's been here the longest."

I said to Hortense, "Did any kid just disappear in Skilly and never be found for years?"

She said, "No, what a strange thing to say. Kids leave to go somewhere else, but they don't just disappear into thin air."

45

I said, "I think the kid was found in the end, but by then he was a skeleton."

Hortense laughed. She said, "Who's been telling you stories?"

I said, "No one."

Then she looked up at the sky in case God was watching. It's what she does when she's thinking how stupid the world is. And then she hugged me so I think it's okay. Hortense has been here even longer than Jimmy, so she knows.

But even if Mrs. Clanks didn't lock someone in a cupboard, I don't want her on my list, and I don't want her to come to my funeral because she's not very nice. She hates being here, and she hates us being here too.

One time her husband came to get her after work. He waited outside in his car. I didn't even know she had a husband, but Hortense said that's who he was. When she got in the car she gave him a proper smile, not like the ones she gives us. She was just so glad to get away from Skilly.

I think Mrs. Clanks probably wanted to be a flight attendant or a trapeze artist when she was a child, and she's disappointed she ended up here. That's why she makes so many rules. She wants everyone else to be unhappy too.

Some Skilly rules:

Don't drop your bags and coats on the floor.

Don't bother adults if they're busy.

Don't fight with sticks.

Don't bother Silas if he's in his garden.

If the toilet paper roll runs out, tell Hortense.

Don't put toilet paper roll down the sink.

Don't run in the house unless something bad happens, like a fire—and if there is a fire, don't run, because you have to walk out of the house in an orderly fashion.

Don't put anything in front of the fire exits, because then you can't get out.

Don't take food up to your bedroom.

Glenda Hyacinth
May 1989

Something amazing happened today! I'm not going to
tell anyone, because it's my secret. I'm so happy, I have to
stop myself dancing around, because when Zac saw me
he said, "What's up with you?" and I'm not telling anyone what's up.

This is what happened.

I dropped a pencil down the side of my bed, and when
I crawled under to get it, a bit of floorboard moved. And
under it was a letter! I've been sleeping above a letter since

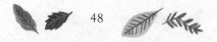

I was nine, and I didn't even know! All I was thinking about was the birds on the roof. It was in an envelope with stars drawn on it and writing that said *To Whom It May Concern*, which means the person who wrote it didn't know the name of the person it was for.

When I found it I could hardly breathe. I didn't know what to do. I sat on the floor and just stared and stared at it. And then I thought, If it's not for someone special, it could be for me, so I opened it. And inside was a letter from Glenda Hyacinth!

It says *1947* on it so it's really old, but the paper isn't yellow or falling apart. It looks like she wrote it yesterday. I don't think anyone ever touched it apart from Glenda and now me. The writing's old-fashioned and neat; all the letters are the same size, and they all lean in the same direction. This is what it says.

24th September 1947

To Whom It May Concern,

I hope whoever finds this letter is a girl. There are too many boys here already. If you are a boy, please put this letter back.

My name is Glenda Hyacinth, and I am eleven years old. I live in Skilly House, which is an orphanage. I don't remember my family,

but I miss them terribly. I especially miss my mother. I hope whoever is reading this has a family and there are no orphanages anymore and everyone has somewhere nice to live.

I got the cane at school today because I didn't know my times tables. I was supposed to recite them all the way to twelve, but I couldn't even remember them up to eight. I had to stand in the corner and practice over and over and I missed my break, and I had to hold my breath so I didn't cry.

The thing I'm best at is handwriting. Even my teacher says so. I hope you think so too. I always make sure the letters touch the lines.

What I like doing best is playing in the bomb site across the road. There used to be a big house there, but now there's only rubble because the Germans bombed it. I pretend the house is still there and I live there and I'm helping my mother cook dinner and lay the table. Once I found a red ribbon and I washed it and kept it and now I wear it, and once I found a photograph of a family, but I didn't keep that. I dug a hole and buried it in the ground.

I also like climbing the tree in the garden. If I could fly, I would climb to the top of the tree and fly away and never come back.

With love from
Glenda

I was so amazed, I read it over and over just to make sure it was real. And all the time I was reading, I kept checking the door in case Zac came in because I don't

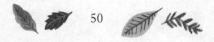

want him to laugh or tell everyone. And now I know the letter by heart. I've always thought about Glenda, and now I feel like I've met her. Then I wrote a letter back.

14th May 1989

Dear Glenda,

I hope you don't mind me writing, but I found your letter under the floorboard. I am a girl, though I share the room with my brother, Zac. I hope that's OK. He always wants to share, but I don't really mind. I think I'd be lonely on my own. I hope you weren't too lonely here. I'm ten and three quarters. Zac's nine.

My real name's Miracle, but everyone calls me Ira. Zac's real name is Zackery.

It's really nice to read your letter. I know your name because it's on the windowsill. You must have pressed really hard, because it's gone in really deep. I think it will be there forever.

I'm sorry you got the cane for not knowing your times tables. If I was hit for getting my times tables wrong I'd be black and blue, but my teacher doesn't hit me for not knowing. She just rolls her eyes.

There isn't a bomb site across the road anymore. There's a block of flats, and lots of people live there. I

don't think they know ghosts are watching them when they're making cups of tea or eating breakfast. There isn't a tree in the garden at Skilly now either. A storm blew it over. Me and Zac saw it. It was amazing.

Skilly House is still an orphanage, but people call it a children's home now. Me and Zac don't have parents either, and I miss them too. Missing them is like a hole in my heart.

I'm going to put your letter back under the floor and I'm going to put this letter there too, and in the future maybe another girl will find them. Maybe by then people will think care kids are special and treat them even better than other kids, and Skilly will be like a palace and everyone will want to go there. Can you imagine it?

I know you must be really old now or even dead, but I'm going to think of you as my friend. You can think of me as a friend too if you like, even if you are a ghost. And if you want to watch me and Zac some-times, that's OK.

Love from Ira

PS Your writing is much better than mine. I can't make all my letters touch the lines. I can't stop them going in all different directions.

Then I got an envelope that was left over from a birth-day card, and I put my letter in it and wrote *Sorry about the envelope* on the back because it was pink. Then I wrote *To Glenda* on the front and put it under the floor-board with Glenda's letter.

And now I feel like I've got a new friend, even though she's a friend from the past. Even though she's probably dead. I've always wanted a special friend, and now I've got one.

City Kids, Country Kids
June 1989

Me and Zac are going on holiday! It's our first ever! All the Skilly kids have been on holiday except us. I don't know if it's because there's two of us and we want to stay together, but we've never been. We've been on outings, just not holidays. Anita took us to the National Gallery in Trafalgar Square to look at the old paintings. I really liked them, but Zac got bored and set off an alarm by going over the rope that stops people from touching them. Afterward we had a picnic in Trafalgar Square and climbed on the

lion statues and fed the pigeons. The pigeons went crazy. All you could see was their fluttering wings and nodding heads.

I've been on a boat on the Thames with my class too. We went under the bridges, and a man told us the history of London and pointed out special buildings. We couldn't see him. His voice was coming out of the ceiling, but I think he was standing on the top. I didn't enjoy it though. I felt so sick, I couldn't look up.

But me and Zac have never been away for a week, or even for a night, and come back. If we ever go away for a night, we don't come back. Ever.

The holiday's organized by City Kids, Country Kids. It's a charity where people who live in the country let city kids stay with them. It's like when country people had evacuees like Silas—only now they don't have to keep them for years; they can keep them for a week and send them back. It's better that way in case they don't like them.

Mrs. Clanks called us into her office. We were worried because kids usually go in there to be given bad news or told off. I've been in twice before today. Once was because I lied to cover up for Zac when he took a packet of cookies from Hortense's tin that was hidden behind the rice in the pantry. Now the tin's behind the cereals on the fridge

and he can't reach it, even standing on a chair. I got into as much trouble for lying as Zac did for stealing the cookies. Mrs. Clanks said if we did that sort of thing we'd ruin our lives. She didn't shout. She just stared at us like she could see how awful we were inside. She made me feel cold.

The other time was when my school report said I was looking out of the window in lessons. Mrs. Clanks tapped her finger on her desk and said, "If you're not careful, you'll come to nothing," which means my life will be wasted. But I think my life's wasted anyway. What sort of life is a care kid's except a waste?

But this time when we went in, she was sort of smiling. It made my heart jump (not in a good way), because I wondered if she was going to send us away and that's why she was happy. She had a yellow ribbon in her hair.

Wearing a ribbon is Mrs. Clanks's distinguishing feature, which means it's the thing that makes her different. If someone didn't know what she looked like, you'd say the woman with the ribbon. It's like burglars wear striped sweaters and Frenchmen have curly mustaches. I don't like it though. It just looks weird. Maybe she wants to look young, but it doesn't work. It makes her look even older.

When we sat down she said, "I have good news. I've found someone to take you for a holiday."

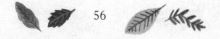

Then she waited for us to say something. But we didn't speak. We were too shocked.

"It wasn't easy to place you together," she said, "but a lady called Miss Freeman will take you. This is a big opportunity. You are going in the summer. I will take you on the train, you will stay for a week, and I will pick you up and bring you back to Skilly."

I felt faint after that. I couldn't work out if I was happy or worried, and I felt dizzy with it. Because going on a train with Mrs. Clanks is the worst way to start a holiday. But then she's going to leave us there, so that's okay.

"You must be polite at all times," Mrs. Clanks said, "and do any jobs required of you, and afterward Miss Freeman will tell me how you've behaved. What do you think?"

I wasn't sure what I was thinking, so I nodded and said, "Thank you."

Zac screwed his eyes tight shut and just sat there. It's what he does when he wants to hide. It's like when little kids put their hands over their eyes and they think you can't see them. Except Zac's nine years old. I'm hoping he'll grow out of it soon.

Mrs. Clanks looked at Zac for a few moments.

Then she said, "Well, off you go then."

I pulled Zac's arm and he followed me out. He didn't

even open his eyes. He was tripping over me. When we got in the hall, he leaned against the wall because he felt wobbly.

He thinks Mrs. Clanks is going to leave us in the forest like Hansel and Gretel and let the animals eat us. I'm worried too. Not about being left in a forest but in case we don't come back.

I told Hortense and she said, "Ira, don't you worry, you'll have a wonderful time. You won't want to come back, but when you do we'll be here."

Silas said, "You'll never forget it, Ira. Take it with both hands."

When he said that, it made me think of Christmas dinner because I always take that with both hands. It's my favorite meal apart from the stuffing. My other favorites are sausages and mash when Hortense cooks it, and fish and chips eaten on a beach when you have to chase the seagulls away. I haven't had fish and chips on a beach yet. It's a favorite for the future.

After I talked to Silas and Hortense, I didn't feel so worried. Then I told everyone else. Esther got a bit huffy, even though she's had two holidays and we've had none. I expect she wants another one. Jimmy's annoyed too. He said, "How long for?" and I said, "A week," and he said, "Oh yeah . . . ," like "yeah" had lots of dots after it, like

we weren't really coming back. And now he's ignoring me. Sophia and Miles wish they were going and Milap said, "That's nice," and Harit said, "I'm going to get you for that!" and chased Zac around the garden.

Ashani's really excited. She said, "You've got to start packing NOW," even though we're not going for weeks, and then she wrote me a list. It said:

What to take on holiday
faverit toy
faverit outfit
faverit thing to do

All the *favorites* were spelled wrong. I didn't say anything. I just gave her a hug and said, "This is for my faverit girl."

I've told Glenda about the holiday too. I told her in my head. I wonder if she ever had a holiday. I hope she's pleased because she can have our room to herself for a week.

Ashani
July 1989

Ashani went to see her new family yesterday. It's the third time she's been. They might adopt her. They've got a garden, and if she goes to live there they'll buy a goal so she can play football. They've got a grown-up daughter who's at university. Ashani met her and said she's nice and wears glasses and green nail varnish, and she smokes so her breath smells funny. Ashani said she likes the family, but last night she came into our room in her bunny pajamas and she was crying. She didn't know why. She just felt all mixed up inside.

I let her sleep in my bed. Zac didn't mind. He doesn't come in my bed now, and anyway Ashani's his favorite. This morning she was back to normal. She did bunny jumps all the way down the stairs while Zac was a fox chasing her.

I hope Ashani's family don't just want to foster her so she has to move again.

Milap and Harit

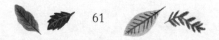

Milap and Harit went to see their mum and dad today. They were so happy. They couldn't stop talking about it. They went on a rowing boat in the park, and then they went to a café. Milap had egg and chips and Harit had egg, beans and chips, and their dad had egg, beans, chips and tomato and their mum wasn't hungry so she just had a cup of tea. It sounded lovely.

But when we were having tea, Milap wouldn't eat anything.

Hortense said, "Go on, have a little bit; you'll be hungry later."

She said it nicely but Milap suddenly jumped up and threw his plate on the floor. The plate smashed and the food went everywhere and it was spaghetti Bolognese, so it made a big mess. Bits of spaghetti were stuck to the cupboards. They looked like worms.

Then Milap shouted, "I hate it here!" and after that he couldn't stop shouting it, like it was the only thing in his head. He shouted, "I hate it here! I hate it!" over and over and then he ran up to his room, and even though he slammed his door we could still hear him shouting.

Harit didn't say anything. He put his hands over his ears and opened his mouth like he was screaming but no sound came out. Not even a whisper. It made me feel awful because I couldn't tell how bad it was, but I knew it must be very bad. It was even worse than Milap shouting out loud.

Hortense took Harit away and Silas sat with us while we finished our tea, except no one did finish it because we'd all lost our appetites. Because if Milap can shout like that and throw his plate and he's really gentle and sweet, it made us think what the rest of us could do. Because we aren't like other people. Other people have all their emotions spread out like all different shades of color, like if you go from red through purple until you end up with blue. But we have our emotions right next to each other so one moment we're happy and then suddenly we're angry and sometimes we don't feel anything at all. It's scary being like that.

Packing
August 1989

Me and Zac go on holiday tomorrow. While we were packing Ashani came in with her Crystal Palace shirt.

She said, "Do you want to take this with you? You can if you like."

She meant me because Zac supports Arsenal.

I said, "No thanks, Ashani. It's too precious."

She looked glad.

Then I said, "I wish I could take you instead," and I tickled her and she laughed and said, "Me too."

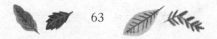

Going on Holiday

Zac felt sick this morning. He said he was too ill to go on holiday.

I said, "You have to go. It's a big opportunity."

He said, "We won't come back, will we?"

I said, "Of course we will. We're only going for a week."

He didn't believe me.

Then I said, "Well, I'm going anyway, even if you don't come," which wasn't true. I'd never go away without him. I didn't think he'd believe me but he did. He stuck out his bottom lip and didn't say another word.

Mrs. Clanks told us to put on our best clothes, the ones we don't normally wear because they're so uncomfortable. Zac wore his white shirt with the collar that digs into his neck and his shorts with the itchy waistband. I wore the green dress I've had since I was nine. It was too big when I got it, and now it's too small. We looked like cartoons with wobbly faces drawn on. Only we didn't look funny.

Hortense gave us sandwiches for the train. Her eyes were shiny, and when I said "Bye," she hugged me really tight. I wanted to stay like that forever. Zac stood completely still when she hugged him, but I knew he didn't want to move either. He wanted to stop time. I wish Hortense could adopt us. I wish she was our mum.

Then I said, "See you," to Jimmy, but he looked away.

We got in the back of Silas's old car that he always has to empty before we get in because he's always picking up junk. Then Mrs. Clanks got in the front. She had a polka dot ribbon in her hair. She didn't say, "Good morning." She just said, "Seat belts on?" After that no one talked. It reminded me of when we came to Skilly.

Silas waited with us at the station. When the train came Mrs. Clanks said, "Coach C, this way," and ran down the platform. I thought her ribbon would fall out. I imagined it lying in the dust, but it stayed in.

As we got on the train Silas said, "Now, don't you forget why you're going—to have some fun."

I had a lump in my throat and it was hurting. Zac pressed his face into Silas's jacket.

"And you, little one," Silas said. "Run and run and use up that energy, eh?"

We got a table on the train. Me and Zac sat one side and Mrs. Clanks sat on the other. Silas put our bags on the rack and said, "I'll see you next week. I'll be waiting for you."

He waved us good-bye from the platform, and we watched him get smaller and smaller until the train turned a corner and he was gone. Zac was nearly crying.

Mrs. Clanks got some papers out of her bag.

"Do you mind if I work?" she said.

We shook our heads because we didn't mind. We were glad. We didn't want to talk to Mrs. Clanks. We never talk to her, except when she tells us what to do, and then we don't talk anyway. She does.

Sometimes we imagine she's a robot and we pretend to be her. We wind her up and do her stony face and make her move faster and faster and crash into things. Zac's really good at it. Even when he falls on the floor, his face stays completely blank. He's really funny.

But I think it's best to be like a robot if you do Mrs. Clanks's job, because whatever happens she always looks the same. You need to be like that when you look after care kids. She doesn't shout and she doesn't cry even when kids are really upset, and her smile's the same whether she's saying "Hello" or "Watch out!" It's the kind of smile you need if you don't know if the news you're giving is good or bad.

As soon as we couldn't see Silas anymore, Zac started wriggling. I got out my sketchbook.

"Do a picture of Mrs. Clanks," he whispered.

I drew her with a tiny head and tiny hands reading a gigantic bit of paper. Zac tried to draw a mustache on her, but I wouldn't let him. He made such a fuss, I shut the book.

"Let's count animals," I said.

London was flying past. It felt like it would go on forever. There were streets and shops and flats and houses and parks, and all of them had people in them. We must have gone past millions and millions of people, but the only animal we saw was an angry dog chewing a bit of wood.

"Boring," said Zac, and he pressed his tongue against the window and began to lick down the glass.

"Zac, don't do that," Mrs. Clanks said.

He didn't hear her at first. He just kept licking. Then he realized she was watching and he put his tongue in. He looked annoyed.

"Please don't do that sort of thing while you're away," Mrs. Clanks said. "I'm sure Miss Freeman won't appreciate it."

There was a smear down the glass like a giant snail trail. Mrs. Clanks gave Zac a tissue, but it wouldn't wipe away. I think you'd need soap to get it off.

I tried to change the subject so we could all stop thinking about it.

"What's Miss Freeman like?" I said.

"I haven't met her yet myself," Mrs. Clanks said, "but I understand she's very nice. She used to be a headmistress, so she's had plenty of practice looking after

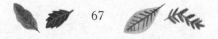

children. She'll be old-school, so she won't put up with any nonsense. You will have to behave yourselves."

Then she looked at Zac.

"Zac?" she said.

She put a question mark after his name. She meant "You will behave yourself, won't you, Zac?"

Zac didn't answer. He just sighed. He didn't even try to keep it inside. He went "Hhhhhhhh" for a really long time. He didn't care what she thought.

I tried to smile because I didn't want Mrs. Clanks to think other kids might be more grateful and then take us back to London. But old-school made me think of Glenda getting the cane for not knowing her times tables. It didn't sound fun at all.

Suddenly, Zac shouted, "Cows!" There was a field of cows, not just one like at the city farm, but lots of them chewing and flicking their tails.

"And sheep," he said, because then there was a field of sheep all walking in a long line like they were queuing up for the best bit of grass.

After that we looked out the window for the rest of the journey. It was so nice. We just ignored the smear on the window. There were farms and fields and rivers and woods and people fishing and walking their dogs and little towns and villages. We saw a big bird fly through

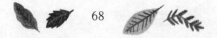

the sky, and we argued about whether it was a crow or an eagle. Zac thought it was an eagle. Then it rained and the raindrops came sideways across the window so they looked like tadpoles racing each other. And when we ate our sandwiches, the sun came out, and there was a rainbow.

By the time we got off the train, I felt all scrunched up, like I'd been stuck in a little box. Zac felt the same. As we stood on the platform he swung his arms around like a windmill. Then he tried to do a cartwheel.

"Please, Zac," Mrs. Clanks said. "Do you want to come back to London with me?"

When everyone had gone, the only person left on the platform was a funny-looking woman with her head pushed forward like a chicken, nodding and bobbing. When she saw us she hurried over. Her hand was stretched out.

"Mrs. Clanks?" she said.

She smiled and looked serious all at the same time, and her voice was soft and high like a child's, even though she was quite old. Mrs. Clanks shook her hand.

"Miss Freeman, pleased to meet you," she said.

"Do call me Martha," said the woman.

She had glasses with silver rims and a chain that went down from her glasses and all the way around her neck in

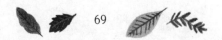

case they fell off. Her hair was brown and speckly gray and it was tied up, but bits were dropping out. She was wearing a yellow dress with no sleeves like a little girl's, and she was very tall and had paint on her dress and big feet like a man's, and she was wearing red sandals. Zac nudged me. I knew he was smirking, but I wouldn't catch his eye.

The woman bent down to look at us. She was a mixture of old and young. She was wrinkly but she had bright shiny eyes like Ashani's. Then I noticed something I've never seen in a grown-up before—she was shy! I've never met a grown-up who's shy. I didn't think grown-ups could be shy because they have to do so many grown-up things. But that's how she looked—shy.

"You must be Miracle," she said.

I nodded. Even though I hate that name, I didn't want to be rude.

"Pleased to meet you," I said, and I gave a little curtsy, like I was meeting the queen. I felt stupid. I knew Zac would think I was an idiot. Martha bowed back.

"And Zackery, lovely to meet you."

Zac scowled.

"Come on then," the woman said. "It's a bit of a drive, but it won't take long. Let me take your cases."

She hurried off, pulling my case and pushing Zac's.

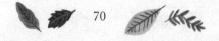

Mrs. Clanks followed her. Then she turned back to us and mouthed, "Come on!" Zac scuffed his feet. He was disappointed already.

"She's just like a teacher," he said.

Appleton House

Martha's town is called Wellsbury. It's not like London at all. The streets have trees on both sides and I only saw one NO POLL TAX sign and no people with placards. There are no sirens either, and no traffic jams.

Martha's house is at the end of a cul-de-sac, which is a street that stops so you can't go any farther. Her house blocks the road so if you kept on driving you'd crash right into it, and it's got sky around it instead of being squeezed into a gap like Skilly.

There's a window above her door and it says APPLETON HOUSE in gold writing. I thought only children's homes and prisons had names. It's nice for a normal person's house to have a name too. It gives it personality. Martha said it's called Appleton House because there used to be apple trees there.

At first I thought loads of people must live there because the coat rack's covered in coats and hats and old-fashioned umbrellas that don't fold up. But it's only

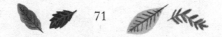

Martha. All the things are hers. There's an old mirror in the hall, with silver coming off so it's like looking into a frozen pond. And there's a black-and-white photo of a man with a beard dressed like a vicar, and wherever you stand it looks as though he's staring right at you. It's like he's reminding you God's always watching. You can't get away from him.

Martha's sitting room is the nicest room in the world. There's a rocking chair with a torn cushion, a lumpy yellow sofa, a footstool covered in roses that have nearly faded away and a table with books and magazines on top. There's a fireplace with dusty bits of coal in it, and there are bookshelves all the way from the floor to the ceiling, and everywhere that's not covered in books is covered in plants and paintings. I was trying to work out why it looks nicer than Skilly even though everything's scruffy, and I think it's because Martha loves it. Skilly looks like nobody ever loved it at all.

But Zac didn't look at the room. He went straight to the window and stared at the garden. It's got a lawn like a bowling green that no kids ever play on, and there are no tall buildings all around. And there are flowers all down the sides of the grass, and at the bottom there's a tree with leaves that go all the way to the ground.

Martha said to Zac, "Do you like it?"

Zac shrugged, which gave the wrong impression. It was because he liked it too much.

"That tree," Martha said, "is called a weeping willow because it looks like it's weeping."

And it did. Its leaves looked like they were tears falling to the ground.

"Why don't you have a look," Martha said.

She opened the windows and they weren't windows at all. They were doors, and you can walk right through them.

"Off you go," she said.

Zac didn't move. He was frozen.

"Can I go too?" I said.

"Of course," said Martha.

I took Zac's hand and pulled him, and suddenly we were running on the grass under the big, blue, perfect sky.

"There's a stream at the bottom of the garden—take your shoes off," Martha said.

But we weren't paying attention. Zac was doing somersaults and I was spinning around and around because my dress was too tight to do anything else in. When we got to the weeping willow, we stood underneath it and looked up. Light was streaming through the leaves. It was like being in a church.

Behind the tree there's a stream that goes under the fence at the bottom of the garden and out into some

woods. Zac crouched on some stones across the stream and pulled a handful of mud out of the water. Then he rubbed it all over his face.

"Zac! You idiot!" I said.

He stuck out his tongue. "What do I look like?"

"Stig of the Dump."

He grinned. It's his favorite book.

"You do it," he said. "Go on."

I shook my head. "I'll watch."

"Okay," said Zac. "I'll catch a fish and you can have it."

He leaned out to where the water was deeper, and then he began to wobble. I knew he'd fall in. That's what he's like. If he wants to do something he will, even if it means trouble later. He had a big smile on his face because he knew he was about to get wet and no one could stop him.

When he fell it was like slow motion. Even the splashes looked like they came up slowly. Then he got on his hands and knees and began to bark like a dog, and then he dipped his head in the water and shook it. He's good at being a dog. He's always wanted one, and he's always pretending to be one. He's had lots of practice.

But even though I was laughing on the outside, a bit of me was thinking, what if Mrs. Clanks and Martha come? Because Zac didn't look like the boy who got off the train. He looked like a different boy. He was covered in mud,

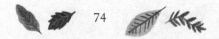

his curls were stuck to his head and his shirt wasn't white anymore. Martha might be shocked to see him.

"Zac, get out," I said.

He shook his head. "Nah-nah-na-na-nah."

But then his face went tight and he wasn't looking at me anymore. He was looking behind me, and when I turned around I saw Mrs. Clanks and Martha coming through the willow. The lines between Mrs. Clanks's eyes were really deep. She was shaking her head, and her spotty ribbon was bobbing from side to side.

"Get out, Zac," she said.

Her voice was extra calm. She must have been really angry.

Zac tried to get out but he kept slipping. In the end I had to pull him. Then he just stood very still and squeezed his eyes shut. Water was dribbling out of his shoes. Martha was staring at him through her silver glasses. She was probably wondering what happened to the nice boy in the white shirt. I crossed my fingers and wished she wouldn't send us home.

"I'm terribly sorry," Mrs. Clanks said. "He's full of beans."

Martha made a little "um" noise.

Then she said, "Why don't you take off your shoes and socks, Zackery, and your nice shirt, and have a play."

75

Zac didn't even open his eyes to take off his socks and shoes. He did it with his eyes shut. It took ages. It was embarrassing. I picked three bits of grass and braided them together so I wouldn't have to watch.

When they walked back to the house, Martha was holding Zac's shoes by the laces and her hand was stretched out like when she met us at the station, only this time it was because she didn't want to get mud on her clothes. Mrs. Clanks was carrying Zac's shirt and her hand was stretched out too, and her other hand was flapping at flies.

Tea with Martha

Me and Zac stayed by the stream for ages, but it was no fun. I kept thinking Mrs. Clanks would take us back to Skilly. I was trying to imagine what expression I could have on my face when we got there to make it less awful. I decided to look like I was pleased to be back and a bit annoyed about the whole experience.

But then Mrs. Clanks came to tell us she was getting a taxi back to the station. She gave us a look and said, "Behave yourselves," and then she went. I took such a deep breath, I felt dizzy.

After that Martha came to get us for tea. She made us wash our hands under a tap in the garden. The water was

so cold I thought my fingers would drop off. It probably turns to ice in the winter. Then she took us up to our room. It was only fourteen steps.

"I'm told you like to share," she said, "but there's a room each if you'd like."

Zac shook his head.

"We'll share," I said.

"Very well," said Martha. "Then this is your room. I hope you like it. Come down to the dining room when you've cleaned up."

Our bedroom looks like it hasn't changed for fifty years, or maybe a hundred. It's got two beds with metal frames and a dressing table with drawers and a mirror shaped like a heart. There's a sink with HOT and COLD written on the taps, and a wooden desk with a lid that lifts up and an inkwell where people used to put ink when they used pens made of feathers. There's faded wallpaper with leaves on it and they're all lined up, and there's a wardrobe that's got the same wallpaper inside, only it isn't faded. I'm going to keep the wardrobe open the whole time we're there so it matches the walls.

Zac put on his shorts and Arsenal shirt, and I put on my jeans and T-shirt. I'm not going to wear the dress again. Not if I can help it. I'm going to leave it here and pretend I forgot it. Before we went downstairs I tried to

wash Zac's face and his hair, because it still had loads of mud in it. The mud got stuck to the sink, though at least he looked better.

You can tell which is the dining room because there's a table and chairs in the middle. There are books and boxes and plants all over the floor, but if you saw the table on its own you'd think you were in a restaurant. There was a tablecloth and there was a teapot covered in purple flowers and matching cups and saucers. The teapot was chipped, so I think the tea set was really old, but Martha loved it too much to get rid of it. There were even little glass pots with silver lids with salt and pepper in them, like you get in cafés. There were napkins too, and sandwiches and sausage rolls and crisps and small tomatoes and chocolate biscuits. It was like a birthday party where there were hardly any guests and someone had forgotten the cake.

Martha was sitting at the table when we went in. She hadn't eaten anything. She was just waiting for us. She was very polite. She said, "Please tuck in." She looked a bit worried, as if the tea wasn't good enough for us. Or maybe it was too good, or maybe she was worried that we'd left mud in the sink.

Zac ate a sandwich so fast it made his eyes water. He just stuffed it in. Then he took another.

"Miracle, help yourself," Martha said. "And drink your tea. It's not too hot."

I didn't want to say we don't drink tea and we've never drunk out of a cup and saucer either, so I put my finger through the handle and lifted the cup really carefully. I pretended I was in an old film and the waitress was waiting to see if I liked it. If I did she would top up my cup with some more. But the tea tasted like warm water. Maybe it's better with sugar like Silas has it. I told the imaginary waitress not to worry. When I put the cup back in the saucer it made a little clink.

After that we didn't talk. We just ate. Zac made a mess like he always does. Hortense says she needs a dog to eat the food he drops on the floor. Crumbs kept falling out of his mouth on to the tablecloth. I had to be extra tidy to make up for him, so Martha might think the mess came from two kids. Martha looked very serious. She was cutting bits off her sausage roll and putting them in her mouth with all different expressions on her face, like she didn't know what to think.

"I do hope you'll be happy here," she said at last.

"It's a lovely garden," I said.

"It's so big," said Zac.

"We have a garden at Skilly," I said, "but we have to share it with lots of other kids."

Then Zac said, "How long have you lived here?"

Martha made a little cough and said, "All my life."

Zac's mouth fell open. It was embarrassing. It was full of food and he didn't shut it. He just kept staring at her. I tried not to stare, but I was shocked too.

"I was born in this house," Martha said. "I lived here with my parents and brother. My father was a vicar. My parents are dead now, and my brother lives in Australia. This has always been my home."

It was hard to understand what she meant. I didn't know someone could live in the same place all their life, right from being a baby to an old person. I'd never even thought of it.

Martha's cheeks went red and then the red went all the way down her neck.

"Please don't worry," she said. "There may be old things here, but there's nothing valuable."

After that everything felt funny in a bad way. I don't even know why. I just felt really bad. Like we'd come to a different planet that we didn't even know existed.

Martha pushed Zac's cup of tea toward him.

"Have a little drink, Zackery," she said.

He shrugged, then he picked up the saucer with both hands, balancing the cup on top. It was fine at first, but when he tried to drink, the cup slid off the saucer and fell

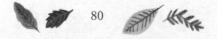

down his front. Tea poured down his Arsenal shirt and onto the floor.

Martha jumped up.

"Oh dear me. Are you burned?"

Zac shook his head. He was looking at his shirt. It was stuck to his chest.

"We don't normally drink out of this sort of cup," I said.

"Of course not," Martha said. "Silly me."

She ran out and came back with some towels.

"There you go, Zackery. Dry yourself down."

Zac looked so sad. He loves his shirt so much he even sleeps in it. Martha began to mop the floor.

"Can I help?" I said.

"No, no, no, Miracle," she said. "Please don't worry."

She was kneeling under the table.

Zac was nearly crying.

"I think we'll go upstairs now," I said.

"Are you sure you've had enough to eat?" she said.

"Yes, thank you. We're full, aren't we, Zac?"

Zac nodded.

"Very well," she said. "Good night."

As we were going upstairs I had a thought, so I ran back.

"Martha?" I said.

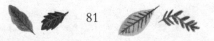

She looked up.

"Yes, Miracle?"

"Could you call me Ira instead of Miracle?"

She nodded.

"And Zackery, Zac?"

"Yes," she said. "Of course."

Her face was very hot and her glasses were falling off her nose. It was lucky she had the chain.

When we got upstairs Zac kicked the wall so hard, he made a dent in the wallpaper.

"Zac, be careful," I said. "She'll send us away."

"I don't care. It's too fancy here. I hate it."

He sat on the bed, and I put my arm around his shoulder.

"Will my shirt be okay?" he said.

"Yes," I said. "We'll soak it in the sink."

We sat there for a while just thinking, and then he said, "I don't really hate it here."

"I know," I said. "It's just different. I think it'll be okay if we try to be good."

And now he's asleep and he looks like an angel, and I wish Martha could see him, because then she'd understand that he's all different things all at the same time. He's clumsy and he always finds trouble and he pretends he doesn't care, but he's also very sweet.

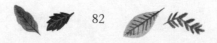

Chickens

I couldn't sleep last night. I was worried we'd upset Martha, and anyway it's too quiet here. There's hardly any noise except for animal sounds, and I don't know what animals they are. Birds, maybe, and foxes. They squeak and yelp and all around them is silence. I tried to picture them in my head, but I couldn't. I just lay there wishing I could hear a siren or traffic or people shouting in the street. Just so I'd know we weren't on our own.

When it was morning I was worried in case Martha wanted to send us back to Skilly. But she said, "Morning, children!" in a singsong voice and didn't seem cross at all. At breakfast there was no tablecloth, and we had mugs and plates that didn't match. I expect she thought it wouldn't matter if we broke one. Me and Zac didn't drink tea either. We had juice.

After breakfast Martha said, "We're going to get eggs for lunch." We climbed over the fence at the bottom of the garden and into the woods and walked along a path. There were so many trees that when I looked up I could only see little bits of sky. Apart from that, it was all green leaves. Zac was chasing squirrels, but they were too quick for him. He couldn't even touch their tails. It's the nicest walk in the world. It was two miles there and two miles back. I don't know if I've walked that far before, but I could have walked forever.

We got to a farm with a field full of chickens. There was a table next to the gate and a saucer with money in it and some empty egg boxes.

"There's no eggs left," I said.

Martha smiled.

"We collect our own."

"What do you mean?" said Zac.

"We collect them from the chickens."

She gave us a box each, and we went into the field. The chickens started squawking when they saw us and ran around making bubbling noises and shaking their feathers. Me and Zac were frightened. Zac kept screaming and jumping around. His eyes were nearly popping out of his head. Martha said the chickens wouldn't hurt us. They were only excited because they thought we were going to feed them. But we kept running away. We couldn't help it.

After a while Martha said, "If you don't calm down, I'll get the eggs myself."

So we calmed down and the chickens calmed down too, and then they were just clucking.

We found eggs hidden under straw in the field and also

84

in the chicken coop, which is where they sleep. Some had feathers stuck on and bits of mud, and most were white, and some were speckled and one was brown. When we filled our egg boxes we had six each, which makes a dozen. Martha put some money in the saucer. She said the farmer would get it later.

I said, "What if someone takes it?"

She said, "Who's going to take it?"

I looked around. There was no one there except us.

"No one," I said.

As we walked back Martha said, "I hear even people in London keep chickens."

"That's the sort of thing Silas would do," I said.

"Who's Silas?" Martha said.

"He looks after Skilly," I said. "He's the caretaker."

Then I said, "He was an evacuee," and Zac said, "He's traveled the world."

We wanted Martha to know how interesting he is.

Later we had eggs with toast fingers. Martha called them *soldiers*. I think it's because she lived in the war. The eggs were really nice. I'd never had an egg that was just laid. Then we played in the garden and Zac fell in the stream again, but he didn't get into trouble so I jumped in too.

But after that things went wrong. Zac climbed the

willow and broke a branch off, and it fell down with all its leaves just lying there.

Martha said, "Do you have to climb everything?" She said it quietly, but that made it worse.

Zac shrugged, which looked not very nice.

Then we fell on some flowers and they broke. Martha took them inside and put them in a jug, but they looked better in the garden, and now they'll die soon.

Later on Zac broke the rocking chair. Rocking chairs are for old people, not kids, so he should never have sat on it. He was rocking really hard. He looked like he was about to take off and then he flew right over the back and one of the rockers snapped. I expect the chair belonged to Martha's parents or grandparents even, and that means it's *priceless*, which means you could never have enough money to pay for it because it's worth more than money. Martha probably sat on it when she was a little girl, so it's full of her dreams.

I was so upset, I had to stop myself from crying. Zac said to keep it a secret but I told Martha because she'd find out anyway, and if we didn't tell her she wouldn't trust us. When she saw it her face went red. Then she put it in the corner and said not to touch it.

When she'd gone Zac called me a snitch.

"I'm not a snitch," I said.

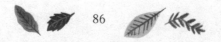

"Yes, you are," he said. "I hate you."

And we had a fight and a cushion got torn and this time I didn't tell Martha. I just turned the cushion over so she wouldn't see it yet, because I thought if she saw one more thing go wrong today she might send us home. If it was on TV people would laugh, but in real life it wasn't funny at all.

At teatime Zac ate really quickly and I kept saying please and thank you and didn't eat much, and Martha hardly ate anything at all. She just looked sad. She was probably thinking if we stay for a week she'll have nothing left that isn't broken. She must be disappointed, especially as she's old-school.

And now Zac's asleep and I don't even want to cry anymore.

I think me and Zac are in the wrong place. It's like if you play a football match on an ice rink, and the players keep falling over. Or if you put a teacher in the jungle, and there's nowhere for the desks and chairs. We're always in the wrong place. Me and Zac don't belong in a normal house—we belong in a *children's home*.

Zac wants to go back to Skilly, but I want to stay here. I'm crossing my fingers and saying prayers in my head in case God's listening, even though I'm not sure if I believe in him.

Reasons to stay:

I want to collect more eggs.

I like the garden.

The house is full of interesting things.

I want to get used to the quiet at night.

We can see stars.

I like Martha.

Martha might like us if she knew us better.

If we go back to Skilly, the others will laugh at us and
Hortense and Silas will be disappointed, and Mrs.
Clanks will be angry and like us even less.

If we can't be happy here for one week, people will
think we can never be happy and no one will want
us for good.

I want to do some drawing in the garden.

Reasons to go back early:

None.

Bats

Me and Zac didn't break anything today. We were extra
careful. We didn't touch anything unless we had to, like
if we had to pick up a cup to have a drink. Martha was
quiet. I kept thinking she wished she'd never invited us
to stay, but she was too polite to say.

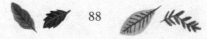

She told us to make ourselves at home, but we didn't feel comfortable in the house so we stayed in the garden. When we came in she kept clearing up after us. She put our shoes into pairs when we left them in the hall, and she picked up our cups as soon as we'd finished with them. You'd think in such a messy house it wouldn't matter where things are but they must be in a special order, even though other people can't tell.

For dinner we had shepherd's pie. It wasn't as nice as when Hortense makes it. Martha isn't the best cook. It's probably not worth cooking for just one person, so she doesn't get much practice. She probably mostly eats sandwiches. Then we went back in the garden.

We had ham sandwiches for tea and little pink cakes called fondant fancies, but I lost my appetite and couldn't eat any. I was waiting for Martha to tell us we were going back to London early. I didn't want to be swallowing when she told us. I kept my fingers crossed under the table. She looked funny—not funny ha-ha, but funny like she was thinking something she wasn't saying. When she finished drinking her tea she put the cup in the saucer and made a little cough.

"Ira and Zac," she said. "I do hope you'll be patient with me."

Her head was bobbing.

"I haven't had children of my own," she said. "I've

89

rather missed out, I think. So I tend to be set in my ways. You two will be an education to me."

I wasn't sure what she meant but I thought she wasn't sending us back to Skilly, so I uncrossed my fingers. Zac took one of the pink cakes, bit off the top and licked out the cream.

"The funny thing is," Martha said, "when I was a headmistress I would speak to hundreds of children at a time, but I don't think I have ever sat down to tea with just two."

She smiled.

"Can you understand that, Zac?" she said.

Zac looked surprised, like if a teacher asked him a question and he hadn't been paying attention. He pushed the whole cake into his mouth so he wouldn't have to answer. Then he started coughing.

Martha's face went all out of shape.

"Spit it out, Zac," she said.

Her voice was wobbly.

Zac spat the cake into his hand. It was all soggy and pink and crumbly. He looked at it for a moment and then he shrugged and put it back on the plate with all the other cakes no one had touched. I felt so ashamed.

At first I thought Martha was crying. Her eyes were wet and her face was all screwed up. But then I saw she

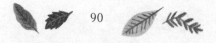

wasn't crying at all; she was laughing. She laughed quietly at first, but then she was laughing really loudly and she was rocking from side to side, and her glasses went lopsided. Zac was laughing too and making faces like he thought he was the funniest kid in the world, and I just thought how stupid everything was and I started laughing as well. And then we were all laughing and looking at the pink blob on the plate.

We laughed for ages. Just when we all stopped, someone started again.

Then Martha said, "Fill up your plates; take what you like. Bring a drink too and follow me."

And we carried our plates down to the stream.

"Now," Martha said, "whatever we spill, the birds will eat."

We stayed out by the stream until it was nearly dark. Me and Zac tried to build a dam, but the water still got through. We told Martha about Skilly and Silas and Hortense and the tree blowing down. She told us about her life with her big brother Douglas and her dad the vicar and her mum who used to make tea for the congregation, who are the people who go to church. It's her dad in the picture in the hall. He's the one who's always watching.

And she told us her full name is Martha Bonita

Freeman. Bonita's a Spanish name. It sounds quite funny next to Martha. It was her gran's name, but her gran never went to Spain. She didn't even like going on holiday. It's a mystery why she was called Bonita. Martha said all families have mysteries.

And she told us one time Douglas found a baby hedgehog, and they fed it bread and milk until it got bigger and then they set it free. It crawled into the grass by the stream, and now she thinks its great-great-great-great-grandchildren might live in the garden.

And she also said she always wanted to prove she was as clever as Douglas because in those days people thought boys were cleverer than girls. That's why she became a teacher and a headmistress. But her real dream was to be an artist, and now she's stopped being a headmistress, and she's got a studio at the top of the house. She said she'll let us see it tomorrow! And then I remembered seeing the paint on her dress when she met us at the station and it didn't seem funny at all anymore; it seemed wonderful.

We all stayed outside really late. When it got dark bats came out and swooped around us, and we sat by the stream and watched and didn't talk at all and everything was perfect.

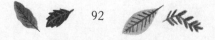

Martha's Studio

Martha's studio is in the attic. It's sixteen steps up from our bedroom and thirty steps from the hall. But apart from being in the attic, it's nothing like our bedroom at Skilly. For one thing, there's no bed or wardrobe because it's not for sleeping or getting dressed in. It's just for painting. A whole room just for painting!

When we went in the smell of paint made me feel dizzy. But when I saw the paintings, I forgot the smell, and all I could think was how amazing the colors were. There are loads of paintings just leaning against the walls. Some are small, but some are even taller than Martha. They're not paintings of things, they're just colors and shapes. One's a red square with yellow and green lines on it, and the lines look like they're moving. I couldn't stop looking at it.

"Did you do these?" I said to Martha.

She nodded. It's amazing to think all those colors are in her head.

"What are they?" Zac said.

"You just have to look," I whispered.

"Look at what?" he said. "What are they?"

"I don't know what they are, Zac," Martha said. "They're feelings, I suppose. You know when you run around and that shows how you're feeling inside—well, these paintings show how I feel inside."

"Can't you paint properly?" Zac said. "Dogs and people and houses and things."

Martha smiled. She didn't seem annoyed.

"Well, yes, I can paint things and I did for a long time," she said. "But now I paint feelings."

"Why?"

"I don't know," Martha said.

She picked up a bit of paper.

"You know, Zac, the older I get the less I ask why. Does that make sense to you?"

Zac shook his head. "No."

"Would you like to paint something?" she said.

Zac shrugged. "Okay."

Martha squeezed three colors onto a bit of plastic she called a palette. It's what artists put their paint on. The colors were red, yellow and blue, and they looked like shiny slugs. Then she gave Zac three brushes.

"Use a different brush for each color," she said. "Paint what you like."

Zac took a brush and stuck it in all the paints and swirled them together until most of the color went brown. Then he painted a big swirly circle on the paper and put some yellow on top and then red and then blue, and he

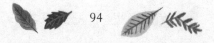

kept making really big lines. He did it fast like he knew exactly what he was doing, and then he stopped. He looked pleased. So did Martha.

"That looks like a painting about feelings," she said.

"No," Zac said. "It's a velociraptor fighting a triceratops."

When it was my turn, I tried to be really careful so the colors wouldn't mix together. It was meant to be a garden, but it wasn't very good. Zac's painting was better. But I was so happy I didn't care.

"If you like," said Martha, "I can set you up in the garden to do some painting."

So that's what we're doing tomorrow!

Painting

There were two easels in the garden this morning with canvases on them, just like artists use. And there was a table with paints and brushes, and they were for me and Zac! I could hardly eat my breakfast. I just wanted to get started.

Zac didn't want to paint, so Martha came in the garden with me and explained everything. She said the paint was acrylic, which means it dries quicker than the oil paint she uses in her studio, so I can take my painting back to Skilly if I like it. It's not as smelly either. Oil paint is what

van Gogh used. Van Gogh was the one who painted sun-flowers and cut his ear off. Acrylic's more modern.

Just as Martha was showing me how to squeeze the paint from the bottom of the tube, Zac shouted from the house. We ran in. He was standing in the kitchen with sugar around his mouth and down his front and all over the floor. The sugar bowl was broken into pieces.

"Zac!" I shouted.

I couldn't help myself. He didn't say anything.

"Go and get cleaned up, Zac," Martha said, and he ran up the stairs.

Martha picked up the broken bowl and swept up the sugar. I tried to help but I kept getting in the way.

"Don't worry, Ira," she said. "I'll sort it out. Go and do your painting."

But I couldn't go. I just couldn't.

I kept saying, "I'm really sorry. He didn't mean any harm."

"I know, Ira," Martha said. "I know."

When I said, "Maybe I should see if Zac's all right," she got annoyed.

"Ira," she said, "you worry too much about Zac. Maybe you should worry about yourself sometimes."

"What do you mean?" I said. My voice sounded really small.

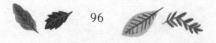 96

"Maybe worrying about Zac is easier than worrying about yourself," Martha said. "You're always thinking about what Zac wants. What I wonder is, what does Ira want? Do you know?"

I couldn't look at her. I had to look out of the window. Silas asks me that sort of thing but no one else does, and with Silas there's never time to talk properly. Someone always interrupts. Martha looked like she was waiting for an answer, like she had all day, but if I told her the truth I would die of shame. Anyway, what I want wouldn't be what I want if I have to ask for it. What I want is for someone to want me and Zac.

I shrugged.

"I don't know what I want," I said.

"Well," she said, "how about that painting you were going to do?"

I felt really bad after that, but when I started painting I forgot. I was just thinking about the colors. I used two different greens and made another green by mixing blue and yellow together. I painted the willow and the lawn and the flowers down the sides, and a little bit of the blue stream poking through the leaves.

And then I saw Glenda under the willow. It really was her. It's the first time I've seen her. She was jumping up and touching the leaves. She looked so happy. She kept

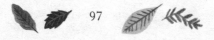

disappearing and then coming back again. I waved to her but she didn't wave back. I didn't mind. I'm just pleased she didn't stay on her own at Skilly. I put her in my painting, very faint so if you didn't know she was there you wouldn't see her. Or you might think she was a dove.

Martha said my painting is impressive, which means not bad for a beginner. I'm going to take it back to Skilly so I can remember this holiday forever.

Paint Colors

Artists' paints have really complicated names. They're not just green and blue and red and yellow. They're all the colors in between. Some of them are colors I never even knew existed. The names are really hard to remember, so Martha said I should make up my own. These are my names next to the proper artists' names.

Cerulean blue	Summer sky
Ultramarine	Stormy sky
Prussian blue	School uniform
Chromium green	Grass stains
Sap green	Martha's lawn
Cadmium yellow	Sherbet lemons
Burnt sienna	Spaghetti Bolognese
Cadmium red	Anita's lipstick

Raw umber	Skilly stairs
Magenta	Pomegranate seeds

Afterward Martha stuck my names onto the tubes of paint. It means Zac can use them too if he wants. Martha doesn't need to.

My Favorite Things

We're going back to Skilly tomorrow. I want to see everyone but I don't want to leave, because then Martha and Appleton House will be a memory. And memories mean things are *gone*. I don't want here to be gone.

I haven't even written in my diary properly, so these are some of my favorite things so I'll never forget them:

Zac found a frog the size of his fingernail and put it in the stream.

We walked to the farm four times. Two times we went just for fun, not even to buy eggs. We're going again tomorrow to get eggs for Skilly. That means we will have walked twenty miles altogether, because we'll have been five times and every time is four miles.

We had tea in the garden four times, even one time when it was raining.

One evening we counted eight bats in one go.

Martha showed us photos of when she was a
    child playing under the willow, and the tree
    was much smaller. Now that she's grown up
    she looks like her mother, the vicar's wife.

We drew pictures on blank cards and sent them
    to Skilly.

I saw Glenda dancing under the tree, and one
    time she was splashing in the stream.

Zac climbed to the top of the willow when
    Martha wasn't looking, and he didn't break
    any branches. He said he felt like a bird.

Doves sit at the top of the willow and they make
    cooing noises, but when Zac climbed up they
    flew away.

I like it being quiet at night now. It's like being
    wrapped in a big, soft blanket.

Martha doesn't go to church, even though her dad was
a vicar. She says God is in the garden.

Back to Skilly

This morning we collected twelve eggs in one long box
to take back to Skilly. Me and Zac aren't frightened of the

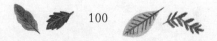

chickens anymore so it was easy. We didn't take the plain eggs. We just took the speckled ones because they're the prettiest. Then we said good-bye to the chickens because we won't see them again. As we walked back we didn't talk at all. Zac just chased the squirrels. I was too sad to talk.

When Mrs. Clanks came to get us, she gave Martha a form with CITY KIDS, COUNTRY KIDS at the top. I wonder if Martha will ever take care kids again.

I didn't want to bring my dress back to Skilly, so I left it in the wardrobe and shut the door. It's the first time the door's been shut all week.

Martha drove us to the station, but she didn't wait with us. I think she wanted to get back to Appleton House so she could have it all to herself. Maybe she wanted to fix the rocking chair and see what else was broken. She said good-bye on the steps. First she shook hands with Mrs. Clanks, and then she leaned down and kissed my cheek. I could see myself in her glasses.

"What do you say, Ira?" Mrs. Clanks said, which was annoying because I was going to say thank you and her saying that made it seem like I'd forgotten.

"Thank you for having us," I said, and then I did a stupid curtsy. I couldn't help it. I don't think Zac saw. He was looking at his shoes. Martha had polished them and the sun was bouncing off them.

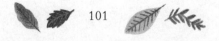

"Thank you," said Martha. "It's been a pleasure."

Then she kissed Zac's hair. She knew he'd jump if she touched his face. He stood really still but didn't move away, so it was okay.

"Zac?" said Mrs Clanks.

"Thank you," said Zac.

Martha had wrapped my painting in newspaper. When she gave it to me she said, "Look after it; it's a beauty."

Then she gave Zac the box of eggs. He wrapped his hands around it like it was a new baby and he couldn't drop it. Probably it was even more fragile than a new baby, like lots of new babies.

I looked back at Martha as we went into the station. She should have looked funny with her big feet and her bobbing head, but she didn't. She looked nice and a bit worried, like she thought Zac might drop the eggs.

All the way back to London, I felt like I'd left a bit of myself at Martha's house. Like part of me will always be a little ghost painting in her garden. Zac held on to the box of eggs the whole way back. He didn't even wriggle.

Mrs. Clanks got out her papers again so we didn't have to talk to her. The only thing she said was, "I think you made a very good impression. Well done."

I felt bad when she said that, even though I think she

was trying to be nice. I expect she's pleased because Martha might let other kids go there.

Silas was waiting at the station like he said he would. It was like he'd been standing there the whole week. He had a big smile on his face. I ran along the platform and gave him a hug. Zac did a funny sort of skip because he didn't want to drop the eggs.

"You look different," Silas said.

"What do you mean?"

"More grown up, I suppose. Like you've seen something of the world, and it's changed you."

I said, "Is that okay?"

And he said, "Oh yeah."

It's strange being back at Skilly. Everything seems so noisy and busy. Someone's hung a sheet on the flats across the road with STOP THE POLL TAX in big black drippy letters. When the wind blows it flaps against the wall. Skilly looks the same though. It looks like we never even left.

Zac gave Hortense the box of eggs. She opened it carefully in case they were broken, but all twelve eggs were perfect.

"Did you carry them the whole way?" she said.

Zac nodded.

"It's a small miracle," she said.

Because miracles can be big or small. Miracle isn't just a name for a kid somebody doesn't know if they want or not. Miracles can be big, like someone walking on water, and small, like eggs not getting broken.

Me and Zac told everyone about our holiday over and over. Sometimes I told a story one way and then Zac told the same story in a different way, but nobody minded. They couldn't believe Martha lived in the same house all of her life. Everyone's mouth fell open. Even Hortense was surprised. We sat at the kitchen table, and everyone listened and looked at the speckled eggs. Ashani sat on my lap and put her head on my shoulder. She seemed a bit sad. She liked the eggs with the feathers on top, so I gave her a feather to cheer her up—a really soft white one. I expect she wishes she'd come.

Everyone liked the cards we sent, and my painting. I didn't tell them Glenda was in it. They all thought the little Glenda shape was a rabbit.

Hortense said, "It's beautiful, Ira. Can we hang it in the hall?"

But I don't want it in the hall. Someone might kick a ball at it or scribble on it. I want it in my room so I can remember the holiday forever.

Hortense said, "Well, I'll just have to come up and look at it sometimes, to get a taste of the country."

We had the eggs with toast, and we told everyone about Martha's toast soldiers. It was nice sitting at the table together, but the more we told our stories the more it felt like they happened a long time ago. Silas must feel like that. He must feel like his stories happened a hundred years ago. Or in another lifetime.

When I saw Jimmy he said, "So you came back then?" and I said, "Yeah. . . ." And this time I put lots of dots at the end of it.

I hope I never forget what Martha looked like or how lovely her garden was or what it felt like to stand under the willow or walk two miles to get eggs or go to sleep when all you can hear is animals in the woods.

The trouble with holidays is they make ordinary life feel even more ordinary.

Ashani's Gone

Ashani left today. She went to live with her new family. It was all arranged while we were on holiday. I think that's why she was sad when we came back. Probably she was happy-sad.

When she said good-bye, she made funny faces and she kept tickling everyone and laughing. I picked her up and held her tight and she wrapped her legs around me

like a monkey. I wished and wished I didn't have to let her go. When she got in the car, she was smiling and waving and sticking her tongue out of the window. But as the car drove away I couldn't tell if she was smiling anymore, but I thought maybe she wasn't and I felt awful.

Zac was annoying all day and I hated him, but then I saw his eyes were red and I thought maybe he was upset because he liked Ashani too. Now everything feels like the sun's gone in and it's going to be cloudy forever.

I told Glenda about Ashani and how bad I feel now that she's gone. I haven't seen her since we got back, but I told her in my head. I keep looking out of the window in case she's in the garden, but she's not there. Maybe she stayed at Martha's.

Silas Is in the Paper
September 1989

Silas has his picture in the paper. He's standing with some other people, and they're holding placards with STOP THE POLL TAX written on them. Some people are holding a sheet with CAN'T PAY, WON'T PAY, and the sheet's drooping onto heads of the people in the middle, but they don't seem to mind. Everyone's smiling like they're having a nice day out. It's not a very good picture of Silas though.

"You look like you're wearing a wig," Hortense said.

And he does. He looks like he's in disguise, like he's a spy or something.

Hortense stuck the picture on the kitchen board and somebody wrote *Who is this man?* next to it.

Back to School

We went back to school today. It's my last year before I go to secondary school. Some of the new little kids were crying because they wanted to go home, and others were running around thinking they were really grown up, when they looked really small and sweet in their tiny uniforms.

I told Amanda and Kaleigh about my holiday. I usually tell them I don't like holidays, but this time I told them about Martha and the chickens and the garden. They laughed when I told them about Zac pretending to be a dog in the stream, and for a moment I felt like a proper friend. I didn't tell them about City Kids, Country Kids. I said Martha was our aunt! Now I'll never be able to invite them to Skilly in case they find out.

We got a new teacher called Miss MacDonald. She's Scottish and she's young and she's got a really nice accent. I really like her already. She's going to teach us French in case we marry someone French or just want to go there on holiday. And we're going to do science and write lots of stories. It's cheered me up having Miss MacDonald as my teacher.

Postcard from Martha

We've got a postcard from Martha! It's a picture of a chicken. She didn't write much because there wasn't much space, but me and Zac know it by heart. She said the house was quiet without us, and it wasn't as much fun collecting eggs on her own, and she hoped we didn't have to work too hard at school. At the end she put *Martha* and a squiggle that might have been a kiss but might just have been a funny loop she does on the end of her name.

"Do you think we'll go back?" Zac said.

I shook my head. "I expect she'll take different children if she does it again."

He looked sad, so I said, "Maybe if we wait a couple of years, we'll get another turn."

And he shouted, "A couple of years?!!"

After that he was really upset. Every time he saw me he said, "I hate you!" and "You're rubbish!" and pushed past me. He was like that all day until he went to bed, and then he said "sorry" really quietly so I could only just hear. I'm going to stick the postcard on the wall next to his bed so he'll see the chicken when he wakes up.

Pip

A new girl came to Skilly today. She's called Pip. She's ten, but she looks eight. She's moved into Ashani's room, but she's completely different from Ashani. She's small and thin and wears a purple jumper that's too big for her, and her sleeves are all soggy and the wool's come undone because she's always chewing them.

She didn't say anything at tea, and she didn't look at anyone. I tried to catch her eye, but it was like she had a wall in front of her face. She looked sad sitting there looking at her wall. She didn't eat. She just chewed her jumper.

Hortense took some food up to her room later. It's against the rules to take food upstairs, but if I was in charge I'd say the rules don't matter because if Pip doesn't eat she'll starve to death. I'm going to try to make friends with her.

The Mouse

We got a computer at school. Miss Campbell showed us. She said one day everyone will have one. It's a big gray box with lots of wires, and the screen lights up and all the letters are on a special board. When she was plugging it in she said, "Now, where's the mouse?" and everyone looked at the floor in case a mouse ran up their legs. But she wasn't looking for a real, squeaky mouse. She was looking for a thing with buttons on it.

It's quite good because it's got games, but the best thing is it's quieter than a typewriter. When you tap the letters they don't make such a noise.

Glenda

Glenda's back. I'm sure she is. I keep seeing her out of the corner of my eye. I'm sure it's her. I can feel her in our bedroom too. I just know she's there. I showed her the chicken postcard, but I didn't tell her about Martha's because she knows what that was like because she was there too. I'm so glad she's come back.

Steps

These are the steps of all the places I've been since I could count. I always count the steps, because then I know that whatever happens, I only have to go that many steps down to get to the ground. And then I'll be outside and I can look at the sky. It makes me feel better.

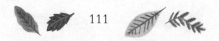

Our bedroom at Skilly	47 steps
Mrs. Clanks's office	2 steps
Martha's studio	30 steps
Our room at Martha's	14 steps
Brenda and Alf's flat	32 steps
Petra's flat	1 step
Our room at Alara's	13 steps
Adam's flat	28 steps
Our bedroom at the Grimbles'	10 steps
Woman who was mean to us	17 steps
Nan in Greenwich	55 steps
Nan next to the garages	3 steps
Auntie with dyed blonde hair	18 steps
Auntie in Brixton	22 steps
The National Gallery	22 steps
Upstairs on London bus	8 steps
Boat on the Thames	12 steps
Dentist	4 steps

Pip's in My Class

Pip's in my class. She walks to school with me and Zac. Well, she doesn't exactly walk with us, she walks behind. It's a bit embarrassing in case anyone finds out she lives with us, because I don't tell people I'm a care kid if I can

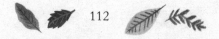

112

help it. But I don't think I need to worry because Pip doesn't speak to anyone. She just sits at the front of the class and looks down, and at break she stands on her own on the playground and won't play.

Amanda and Kaleigh tried to be friendly with her, but she didn't even look at them. She just chewed her sleeve. She wears her old jumper everywhere, even to school. She won't take it off. She won't even let Hortense wash it. Some people might think she's spoiled, but I think she's sad.

Dogs

Zac got a book from the library called *Dog Facts for Dog Lovers*. I don't think I'm a dog lover because I wouldn't have chosen that book, but Zac is because he talks about dogs all the time and wishes he had one, and sometimes he strokes the pictures.

He said, "Do you think our dog's still alive?"

He meant the one in the photo.

I said, "I doubt it."

He got annoyed and wanted to check, so Hortense got out our Memory Book and we opened it to the photo and tried to work out what type our dog was, because the book said how long dogs live depends on what kind they are.

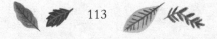

This is some examples of how long some dogs live. How long they live is called their lifespan.

Beagles	12 to 14 years
Boxers	11 to 14 years
Bulldogs	8 to 10 years
Chihuahuas	15 years or more
Dachshunds	12 to 14 years
German shepherds	10 to 12 years
Golden retrievers	10 to 12 years
Great Danes	6 to 8 years
Labradors	12 to 14 years
Poodles	12 to 14 years
Pugs	12 to 14 years
Rottweilers	8 to 10 years
Yorkshire terriers	12 to 15 years

If our dog was a Labrador, it could live for fourteen years or maybe even longer if it's well looked after.

But our dog doesn't look like any of the dogs in the book. It's got big ears and a long nose and little eyes, and it's hairy. It's hard to tell, but it might have thin legs. Hortense said she thought it was a mongrel, which is two sorts of dogs mixed together, and Zac said that was okay because the book says *Mongrels make wonderful companions and are just as lovable as pedigree dogs.*

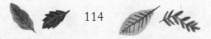

Then he said, "That's a puppy; in the photo. It's a puppy."

I said, "It's not a puppy; it's grown up. Mum wouldn't get a puppy after we were born. You don't get a dog when you've got babies. It's too much work."

"She would," Zac said. "To help look after us."

"You don't get a dog to look after children," I said.

"You can," said Zac, "if you can't look after them yourself."

Then he went quiet and his face was like a sand castle, all sliding out of place, and I couldn't tell if he was crying because my eyes went all blurry and my face was like a sand castle too. I had to take a deep breath and wait for the moment to end, and in that moment I thought maybe our mum kept the dog but got rid of us.

Then Zac said, "That's why I like dogs. Because a dog looked after us."

He said it like suddenly everything made sense, but he didn't look like everything made sense. He looked like nothing made sense and he hated everything.

I wish wish wish wish we knew why our mum left us and who she was and where she is. Because not knowing anything means anything could have happened and whatever me and Zac imagine might be true.

Sometimes I think the dog ran onto the road and Mum ran too and they both got run over, or maybe she married

someone who liked dogs but not children. Zac thinks she was a spy and the dog had a microphone hidden under its ear, and then she had to go back to her own country and really we're foreign. When he was little he thought she was a prisoner and he would rescue her, but then he had nightmares, so I told him she definitely wasn't a prisoner. He made me cross my heart and hope to die, so I hope I wasn't wrong.

What I really think is that she's probably ordinary like us and has bobbly old cushions on her chairs and dust in her hall like most people do. And then I feel angry with her for being mysterious, when probably she's no different from anyone else. Except most people don't leave their children. So that makes her different, I suppose.

Anyway, we couldn't decide what the dog was, and Hortense said we should think of it as an average dog with an average lifespan, and that's about ten years. So if it was a puppy in the photo, it might still be alive, and if it was an old dog, it probably died of old age. That is if it didn't get run over.

Alice
October 1989

Pip spoke to me today. It's the first time ever. She was leaning against the tree talking to herself, and I thought she might be talking to a ghost, so I went and sat beside her. I was going to tell her about Glenda.

At first I didn't say anything, and then I said, "Who were you talking to?"

And she said—really quietly in a tiny little voice so I almost couldn't hear—"My sister."

I said, "Is she staying somewhere else?"

And she shook her head and said, "No. She's dead,"

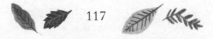

and her face was really flat like it was all so horrible inside her head she had to switch everything off, and then I understood why she has a wall in front of her face.

I wanted to cry but I didn't, because it's her that should be crying, not me, so I took a deep breath like I was about to have an injection. My throat hurt because there was such a big lump in it.

"What's her name?" I said.

She said, "Alice. She's twelve."

After that all the words went out of my head, so I just sat there. I don't think Pip minded. We sat like that for ages and didn't say anything, and Pip chewed her sleeve.

Then I said, "Is that her jumper?"

And she nodded and got up and walked away.

Pip's sister dying is the saddest thing in the world. If Zac died, I'd die too. My heart would stop beating, and I wouldn't live a moment longer. I wouldn't even know how to breathe. It makes me afraid to think about it in case it happens. I know it won't make a difference, but I feel like it might. It's called being superstitious.

Usually Zac is superstitious, not me. If I tell him about Pip's sister he'll think I'm going to die, so I won't tell him. He already thinks something bad will happen if some-one puts up an umbrella in the house or walks under a ladder, and if he's worried about something at school he tries not to stand on cracks. We can be walking along as

if everything's normal, and suddenly he shouts, "Don't stand on the crack," and I have to jump to make sure I miss it. Or if I did stand on it, I have to go back and walk along that bit of pavement again, but this time not stand on it.

I tried to explain that superstitions are made up by people and they're not real, but he said even if people made them up they're still real.

I said, "Yes, but they're not magic; they won't come true."

He said, "How do you know?"

And when someone says, "How do you know?" and you can't prove it, you can't really say anything.

Me and Zac made up our own superstitions. These are some of them:

Changing how you part your hair.

Eating green and red food on the same plate (e.g., lettuce and tomatoes). This means we can't eat salad.

A hedgehog getting run over (that was Zac's idea, but I don't think it's a superstition—I think it's just bad luck for the hedgehog).

Wearing socks that don't match.

Falling out of bed.

Looking at your reflection in a window.

Putting your pants on back to front.

The Wall
November 1989

Miss MacDonald told us about a city called Berlin that's got a wall going right through the middle so people can't go from one side to the other. It's called the Berlin Wall. It's been there for nearly thirty years, which is almost forever. Some people have been stuck on the wrong side their whole lives. If they were out shopping when the wall was built they'd be stuck without their families forever. They can't even climb over because soldiers would shoot them.

I think it's like being a care kid. There's a great big

wall and your family's behind it, but you can never climb over. The only thing you can do is not look at the wall too much, because if you do, you can't think about anything else. Like Pip. You just have to pretend it's not there and get on with everything else.

But Miss MacDonald told us now people are breaking the wall down. It's amazing. She showed us some film. She said it's a historic moment, like when the tree blew down. People were smashing the wall with hammers and putting bits in their pockets and climbing onto it and waving from the top and jumping over to the other side. They were crying and smiling and laughing all at the same time and looking for the people they'd lost, and some people recognized them even though they're really old now.

And the soldiers weren't even shooting because there were too many people to shoot, and they probably wanted to go over the wall too. They probably have aunties or grandmas on the other side.

It was so amazing!

Photo of Glenda

I've seen a photo of Glenda! Hortense found a box of photos of Skilly kids and tipped them out onto the kitchen table. It was like looking at hundreds of ghosts. We knew

they were Skilly kids because they're sitting in front of Skilly House or under the tree before it was blown down. One picture is so old it's brown and white, and the girls are wearing long dresses and they all look miserable, but Hortense said in the olden days people had to sit really still for a long time when they had a photo taken, and it's hard to smile for a long time, so they might not be sad at all. They might just look that way because of all the waiting. Me and Zac tried smiling for a long time and after a while it didn't look like a smile at all. It looked like a scream.

The photo with Glenda isn't as old as the brown and white one, but it's in black and white because they still didn't use colors then. There are seven children in the photo, standing in a row. All the girls are wearing skirts and all the boys are wearing shorts, and all the kids have their socks falling down. On the back of the photo it says *1948*, which is the year after she wrote her letter. The names of the children are written in order, and the last person in the row is Glenda Hyacinth! She's standing next to a boy called Bill Glover. I couldn't believe my eyes. I stared and stared at her.

She doesn't look exactly how I thought she would. She's got long hair and bangs, and she has a ribbon in her hair. I expect it's the ribbon she found on the bomb site. The ribbon's slipped a bit, and it looks like it's going to fall

off at any moment. She's not smiling, though she could have done because it was 1948 and cameras were better then, but she's looking at the camera and her face is all flat. She's probably fed up waiting for Bill to stop talking or for everyone to get in a line, or maybe she's fed up of waiting for life to get better. Or maybe she doesn't want to move in case the ribbon falls off.

Mrs. Clanks stood behind me when I was looking at the photo. I felt a bit awkward, so I said, "What happened to them?"

She didn't say anything for a moment. She just looked at the picture.

Then she said, "They grew up," and she walked away.

She made me feel stupid. Hortense patted my arm.

"It's lovely you're interested, Ira," she said. "These children were here before you. It's lovely you can see their photos."

Now I can imagine Glenda properly. I've seen her running through Skilly and I saw her in the garden at Martha's house, but I never got a good look at her. Now I can really imagine her. I wanted to put a ribbon in my hair too, because we're friends, and friends do that sort of thing. But I haven't got a ribbon, so I put a hairband on instead.

Zac said, "What you wearing that for?"

But I didn't tell him. I just shrugged.

My Story

At school today Miss MacDonald told us about Scotland. She said there's lots of countryside and mountains and lots of rain, so things grow really fast, like enormous carrots, and there's lots of potatoes called tatties.

She showed us tartans, which people make kilts out of. Each family has its own tartan, so people know if they are a Campbell or a MacDonald just by looking at their clothes. It made me wonder if anyone in our family is Scottish and if so what their tartan is. Maybe they're Campbells. If they're Scottish, I hope their tartan's got lots of green in it. Green's my favorite colour.

While Miss MacDonald was talking, some people climbed up the lampposts outside the school and hung a sheet between them with No Poll Tax written on it. It was amazing how they did it so quickly. They just slid right up the poles and down again, and Miss MacDonald didn't even notice. I expect they've done it lots of times before.

Afterward Miss MacDonald got us to write stories. She said to use our imagination and write about something from the past. She says a good imagination can make something ordinary extraordinary.

124

I wrote about a ghost called Glenda who never grows up but is always dreaming about what she might become. It's based on my Glenda, but it's not really her. Miss MacDonald liked it so much she wrote on the bottom of my page *Ira has been working hard and has written a beautiful story. She has a wonderful imagination.*

At the end of school when everyone had gone, she said, "You've quite a talent, Ira," and she told me to show it to Mrs. Clanks. I didn't want to, but because I nodded I had to, so when I got back to Skilly I went to see Mrs. Clanks.

After she read Miss MacDonald's note, she said, "Well done, Ira. Shall I read your story?"

I wanted to say no because she's not the sort of person who believes in ghosts, but she wasn't asking me as a question. Her face went funny when she was reading it. She didn't like it at all, even though it's not very long. When she finished she put it on her desk.

"Who is Glenda?" she said.

"She's a girl in the Skilly photo that's got nineteen forty-eight on the back," I said. "She used to live here."

Mrs. Clanks said, "I see."

Then she said, "Perhaps you should write about people you know—real people, not imaginary ones."

"She is real," I said.

"What I mean, Ira, is it would be better if you lived

125

in the real world. Keep your feet on the ground. Don't dream your life away."

I felt horrible when she said that.

"The real world's no fun," I said.

"You had fun with Martha, didn't you?"

I said, "Yes, but I'm at Skilly now, and it's no fun here at all."

Then I picked up my story and walked out. Just like that. It wasn't even true what I said, but I wanted to hurt her feelings like she hurt mine. When I came upstairs I tore my story into lots of pieces and threw them in the bin. They looked like confetti that you throw at a wedding, only instead of happy confetti, they were sad confetti, like you might throw at a funeral.

I hate writing, I hate drawing, I hate everything. I don't ever want to grow up and be like Mrs. Clanks, but I don't want to be a child either.

Ghosts

I couldn't sleep last night. I was too upset about my story. Even imagining an owl on the roof didn't make me feel better. I got out of bed and looked out the window. There was a big moon in the sky, and I was just thinking how lovely it was when I saw Glenda. She was running

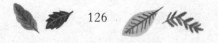

through the garden and she looked really happy and free, and I wished I could be outside with her.

And then I thought, Why can't I? I can if I want to.

So I decided to go out too.

Zac was asleep. His foot was sticking out from the blanket and it kept twitching. He was probably dreaming about playing football. I opened the door really quietly and crept down the stairs. I didn't make a single sound because me and Zac have learned where the creaks are. We did it by pretending we'd get blown up if we stood on a creak. You learn really quickly if you think you might be blown up.

When I got downstairs I unlocked the back door and crept outside. It was quite light because of the moon, but it felt really scary. The grass was cold and wet on my feet.

Then I saw the bushes move so I whispered, "Glenda! Glenda!" but she didn't come out. I was just thinking I'd go back in, but then I saw her running through the garden. She looked like a little wisp of smoke.

And then I noticed lots of leaves were shaking as if children were running their fingers over them, and I realized the garden was full of ghosts, all running around and touching the leaves. So I began to run too. I ran along the trunk and jumped off the end, and then I ran around the

pond and peered into the water and saw the reflection of the moon and insects jumping across the top. And all the time I was running, my fingers were touching the bushes. It was so nice.

But then suddenly the garden felt scary again, so I ran back inside and locked the door, and even though I was scared, I raced all the way up the stairs without making a single creak.

I felt better after that, because now I know that, while we're asleep, Glenda's playing in the garden with the other kids who used to live here. And that makes me feel less lonely.

Zac hadn't moved when I got back to our room. Even his foot was still twitching. He looked so warm, I climbed into bed with him, and when he felt my cold feet he curled up and rolled over.

Mrs. Clanks

I had to go to Mrs. Clanks's office again today. I didn't look at her when I went in, and I wasn't going to listen either. I just hoped she hadn't seen me in the garden.

She told me to sit down, and then she said, "It was very rude of you to walk out when we were talking."

I said, "I'm sorry," even though I didn't mean it.

"Actually," she said, "I wanted to apologize to you. I'm sorry if you thought I didn't like your story. I liked it very much."

She looked strange. Her face didn't look stony anymore. It looked like it was bubbling out of shape.

"What I was trying to say was," she said, "what I've learned in life is that the only way to make things happen is to live in the real world, to make the best of it. Do you know what I mean?"

"To grow up?" I said.

"Yes. That's one way of putting it. Not to live in a dream. If you live too much in your dreams, you will always be disappointed."

I shrugged.

"But I was very impressed with your story, Ira. You must show Silas. You know how he loves a good story."

"I tore it up," I said. "I tore it into a hundred pieces and threw it away."

Mrs. Clanks looked away. It was like she'd cry if she spoke. She made her face even harder than usual and kept swallowing, like she was trying to stop the tears coming.

She said, "I'm sorry if I made you destroy your story. I'm sorry if I was too harsh. Will you write another?"

I was going to say, "No, I won't, never again," but then she said, "One thing you'll learn as you get older is adults

are often wrong—maybe you will be one of those people who is able to live in their dreams."

I felt like crying too, but I wasn't sure why.

I just said, "Okay," and she said, "Very well."

Then she said, "You have a talent. It's quite special. Not everyone is so lucky."

I nodded.

Everything feels funny now. Like it's upside down. I like it better the right way up. Then I know what's happening.

I wonder if Mrs. Clanks did bring the Easter eggs.

Invitation from Martha!
December 1989

Martha's invited us to stay for New Year's! She didn't even arrange it through Country Kids, City Kids. She just did it because she felt like it, and that means she wants us to come. Even though we made lots of messes, she wants to see us again. Me and Zac can't stop smiling, and Zac's jumping all over the place. He'd better calm down before we get there.

When I told Silas he said, "Seize your moment, Ira, seize your moment."

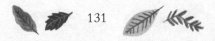

Everyone's happy for us this time, even Jimmy. I expect because he knows we'll come back. The only person who didn't seem happy or sad or anything at all was Pip. She just stared at her wall.

Christmas Tree

We put up the Christmas tree today. Silas got the biggest one he could find. I thought he'd have to cut the top off to make it fit under the ceiling, but it was okay. Jimmy helped him carry it in. They put it in a bucket of water, even though it's already dead. Water keeps it looking alive longer. It makes it think it's still alive.

Hortense got out the decorations, and we hung them on the tree. Pip was really happy. She couldn't help it, even though she doesn't want to be happy ever again. She kept touching all the shiny things.

Sophia decorated the top of the tree because she's the tallest apart from Jimmy, and he didn't want to help. He only wanted to carry it in. Her bit looked best because she didn't put too many baubles on it. Hortense said she's more sophisticated. That means she knows when to stop. Esther got one of her dolls, and Hortense wrapped it in tinfoil and Sophia put it on the top like a fairy. There were so many baubles on the bottom, you could hardly see the branches, but when Hortense put the fairy lights on it all looked lovely. We stood in the dark and stared at it for ages. It felt like magic.

Jimmy

Jimmy keeps disappearing. He's too big to lock in a cupboard, so I think he just goes out. He doesn't want to be at Skilly anymore. He wants to be grown-up. He's so tall, his ankles always stick out of his trousers, and he's got pimples, so I think he feels bad on the outside now as well as on the inside. He might be trying to find his family, or he might just want to get away from us.

Christmas makes care kids feel bad because it reminds us we haven't got a family and other kids have. All the ads have perfect families laughing and pulling Christmas crackers and eating toffees their granddads gave them. Hortense says they're not real families at all, they're just actors, but they still look happier than care kids. I don't feel sad at Christmas though, because all my Christmases have been in care, so I don't know any different. At least the ones I remember. But Jimmy feels sad. Jimmy doesn't like Christmas at all.

I asked if he'd play with us today, but he shook his head and didn't even look at me. Then he went out. He didn't

133

come back until we were going to bed. Mrs. Clanks told him off and Silas said, "Come on, lad," and Hortense gave him a hug and made him some supper because he hadn't eaten anything.

Hortense says teenagers need family more than anyone else, which is a shame because teenagers are the least lovely sort of kid.

Christmas Day

Today I got colored pencils, a sketchbook, felt-tip pens and a slap bracelet, which is what everyone has at school. We all got slap bracelets. Mine's green, Zac's is red, Esther's is yellow. They look like rulers, but when you slap them on your wrist, they turn into bracelets. I also got marbles and a little teapot that opens up into a house. There's a bedroom inside with two tiny beds, and a kitchen with a cooker and a sink and a table and a toilet, and there are three little badgers—mum, dad and baby. Mum badger's wearing an apron and Dad badger's wearing jeans. The baby's wearing a T-shirt and shorts. I wanted to make the dad wear the apron and the mum wear the jeans, but the clothes are stuck on. It doesn't matter though. I still love it.

Zac got the same as me, but instead of the sketchbook

and the teapot, he got a bow and arrow and a Batman model. He's really happy. He's wanted a Batman for ages. Esther got yellow plastic shoes and a bag, and Miles got a Game Boy and some tools, and Jimmy got a portable CD player. It's got plugs he puts in his ears so he can walk around and listen to his music without us hearing or him hearing us. It's good because he doesn't like dance music anymore. He likes bands that scream because that's how he feels inside. Sophia got a CD player too, and Milap got a magic kit and Harit got a Batman like Zac. Pip got a new jumper, but I don't think she'll wear it. I think she'll just keep wearing her old one. She also got a craft kit and lots of sequins and tinsel because Hortense saw how much she loved the shiny things when we did the tree.

At dinner we had red napkins and pulled gold Christmas crackers. The little prizes kept falling on the floor. We had to get under the table to look for them. It was very funny. Zac got a plastic ring he didn't want, and I got a key ring. He wanted to swap, but I wouldn't. I'm going to keep the key ring for when I've got my own door key, even if I have to wait until I'm grown up. Hortense got a fluffy hair clip she put in her hair, and Silas was wearing a paper hat that kept slipping over his eyes. Mrs. Clanks came too. She was wearing a ribbon that looked like holly with two red berries.

I always think Christmas dinner is the best one I ever had, and this year's was the same. I gave my stuffing to Silas because he loves it and I hate it, but I had seconds of everything else. Milap and Harit were the only ones who didn't eat. They just pushed their food around their plates because they wished they were with their mum and dad, and that made them lose their appetites. We read jokes from the crackers to cheer them up, but most weren't very funny. The best ones were:

Why did the raisin go out with a strawberry?
Because it couldn't find a date.

What do you get if you sit under a cow?
A pat on the head.

Glenda came to Christmas dinner too, but no one knew except me. They couldn't see her. She didn't sit at the table because she couldn't eat anything, but she kept popping up all over the place.

After dinner I gave Hortense and Silas some drawings I did in the garden. I gave Mrs. Clanks a drawing too, because since she said sorry for telling me off about my story I've thought of her a bit differently. And when I gave it to her, she gave me a kiss. Zac had a big smirk on his face.

I gave Zac a box to keep dead insects and stuff in. I made it out of a box I covered and painted a hen on. The hen looks like a dog, but he likes it. He loves dogs anyway. He gave me peppermint creams he made with icing sugar and green coloring and mint flavor. The first one was nice, but the second one tasted like toothpaste.

Back to Martha's

We've come back to Martha's! We came on the train with Mrs. Clanks, and we weren't even nervous. We just felt happy. Martha was waiting on the platform. She was wearing a fluffy green coat and orange earmuffs and big boots. I had to stop myself running to her in case I looked too keen and embarrassed myself. When she came up to us she gave a little bow.

"Ira, Zac," she said.

She was smiling.

Mrs. Clanks didn't come to the house this time. She chatted to Martha and then she waited for the next train back to London. When we went she said, "Have fun."

On the way to the house, Martha said, "I was going to get a Christmas tree this year, but I wasn't able to, so I do apologize. You'll see why when we get there."

I tried to think why she couldn't get a tree. I wondered

if she'd lost her decorations. I even thought maybe her roof had fallen in because the house must be very old, but when we arrived the roof looked fine.

But when we got out of the car I heard barking and when Martha opened the door, a puppy jumped out. Me and Zac screamed when we saw her, and she jumped all over us and licked our faces. She's brown and white with floppy ears and big black eyes like marbles, and she's a spaniel and she's four months old and she's Martha's. And she's the most beautiful puppy I've ever seen.

When Zac saw her he was like a puppy too, jumping up and down and rolling on the floor. I felt all soft inside. I kept saying, "Oooh."

"She's called Dash," Martha said.

"Because she dashes?" I said.

Martha nodded. "She doesn't stop. She's wearing me out. I'm glad you two are here."

Me and Zac played in the garden with Dash all afternoon. It was really cold, and she was wearing a little tartan coat that buttoned up under her tummy. Martha said it's just for this winter, as she's a puppy. I don't know if she's Scottish, but it suited her anyway. She's so funny. There's an icicle hanging off the tap in the garden where the water drips. She kept licking it and yelping. She wouldn't stop. She couldn't work out why the water was hard.

Martha gave me and Zac some earmuffs like hers.

Mine are purple and Zac's are blue. Zac didn't want to put his on because they're very big and fluffy, but then his ears got cold so he had to. I tried not to laugh.

Dash makes even more mess than we did when we first came to Martha's. She digs up the plants and breaks things, and she peed on the kitchen floor. Martha keeps mopping up after her.

I think about her all the time. She reminds me of the dog in our photo because even though she's completely different, she's still a dog.

Our black dog compared to Dash:

Our dog
Big
Black
Probably not a puppy
Thin legs
Wet nose
Jumping
Good with children (because you wouldn't put a big
    black dog on a chair with two small children if he
    wasn't)

Dash
Small
Brown and white

Puppy
Short legs
Wet nose
Jumping
Good with children

Martha took some photos of us playing with Dash. She's going to send them off to be developed tomorrow. They should come back soon, and then she'll send us the best ones. I can't wait to see them. I hope Zac wasn't moving.

Later when I opened the wardrobe in our room, my green dress was still hanging next to the leaf wallpaper. I took it downstairs when Martha wasn't looking and put it in Dash's basket under her blanket. Now it's extra comfy.

New Year's Eve

It's New Year's Eve already! The whole week's nearly gone.

Martha said, "Time's gone in a flash," and it feels like that. Like it was a firework, lovely for a moment and then gone. It's New Year's Day tomorrow, and after that we have to go back to Skilly.

We've taught Dash loads of tricks. If we throw a stick

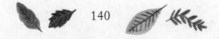

and shout "Fetch!" she'll bring it back, and when we say "Sit," she sits up and holds her paws out. Zac taught her how to run along next to his ankles. When he slows down she slows down, and when he goes fast she goes fast too.

She falls asleep on my lap sometimes, and I have to sit very still because I don't want to disturb her. It's like when Silas had the snake in his sleeping bag, except it feels really, really nice. She's not allowed upstairs, but in the morning she barks until we come down. She's always awake before us. It's like she waits for us all night.

I've done an abstract painting, which is a painting about feelings. Martha left all my paint names stuck on the tubes, so it's easy to remember which color is which. My painting's got lots of greens and blues in it. I did it when I was happy, so it's about being happy. Martha kept looking at it, and then she cleared a space for it on the mantelpiece to keep it safe. She said she'd wrap it up really well so I can take it back to Skilly, but I said it was my Christmas present for her.

When I said that her mouth went funny and she fiddled with her glasses as if they were about to fall off, even though she had her chain. Then she said, "Well, in that case you'll have to come back and do another one."

So we're coming back at Easter!!!

New Year
January 1990

Today's the first day of the first month of the first year
of the 1990s! It's a whole new decade. I was awake when
the New Year happened. Nothing really changes that you
can see, but it felt different.

Martha said if we were still awake at midnight, we
could go downstairs. Zac's eyes just flopped shut as soon
as he got into bed. He couldn't stop them. I kept myself
awake by thinking about my impossible dreams.

One of my impossible dreams is to be an astronaut so

I can look at the world from a long way away, like from the moon. The world must look beautiful from far away, where you can't see all the things that go wrong. You can just see the blue sea and the mountains and the trees and the grass. Another impossible dream is to fly to the top of the willow and sit with the doves. Another is to go back to when Glenda was a little girl and play on the bomb site with her. Another is to make things happen by thinking about them like Matilda does. I've got loads of other impossible dreams, but those are my favorites. I've got ordinary dreams too, like going in a black cab or eating fish and chips on a beach.

When it was very late, Martha put her head around the door.

"Still awake?" she whispered.

She let me borrow her soft, fluffy, yellow dressing gown. Esther would love it. Then she made some hot chocolate and we sat on the sofa and drank it and watched TV. The program showed what was happening in different places in the world. There was a big party at the Berlin Wall. Thousands of people were there, sitting on the wall and waving flags, and there were fireworks, and other people were still pulling the wall apart and smashing it because it goes on for miles. Some people were crying and some were dancing and some were looking for their relatives, but there were too many people so I don't think they could have found them. Everyone looked like they were in a dream. Like a day had come they never imagined.

Martha said, "This is one New Year's they'll never forget."

I thought, This is one I'll never forget too.

After that the program showed a big crowd of people in Trafalgar Square in London. They were singing and sitting on the lions and splashing in the fountains even though it was really cold. I couldn't see any pigeons, but I think they'd gone up into the tall buildings to keep away from the noise. They were probably looking down in case anyone dropped some food. Then it showed a party in Scotland with people in kilts singing and playing bagpipes. Miss MacDonald might have been there, but I couldn't see her. Scottish people love New Year's. They organize the parties.

When it was ten seconds until midnight, there was a countdown. It was like when a rocket goes to the moon. Everyone counted ten, nine, eight, seven, six, five, four—right down to zero. Me and Martha joined in for three, two, one, and when it reached zero they all cheered and kissed each other, and Martha gave me a hug.

"Happy New Year, Ira," she said.

It's the best New Year's I've ever had. I'm going to

remember it for all the New Years in the future when I'm on my own or just with Zac and for all the other decades when I'm old and it's even the next century. At the Scottish party everyone sang a song called "Auld Lang Syne," which is about old friends, and I thought about everyone at Skilly and Zac sleeping upstairs and I felt really happy.

When I came back to bed, I looked out the window and saw Glenda skipping around the willow under the stars.

I hope the 1990s will be better for me and Zac. I hope it'll be like when the Berlin Wall came down and we'll get to see our mum and everyone will be happy.

And when we get to the end of this decade, I'll be twenty-one. And even if we don't meet our mum, it won't matter so much because we won't be care kids any more. We'll be grown-ups. And there'll be robots to do all the jobs, and I might be able to fly or go to the moon, and my dreams might not be impossible.

New Year's Resolutions

Martha's New Year's resolution is to worry less. She says she spends too much time worrying, and it doesn't help. I feel like that about crying. That's why I don't do it anymore.

I've made three resolutions. I could have made ten, but I wouldn't be able to remember them all. My first resolution is the same as Martha's. Second, I'm also going to do more drawing so I get really good, and third, I'm going to concentrate more at school so Mrs. Clanks doesn't tell me off.

Zac said his resolution was to eat more sweets.

I said, "That's not what New Year's resolutions mean—they're supposed to be about being a better person."

So then he said, "Okay, my resolution is to keep my feet off the chairs."

I said, "I bet you can't do it even for one day."

Then he said, "I have a real New Year's resolution, but I'm not telling you what it is."

Then he was all smug like he had a secret. It was quite annoying. But I didn't ask him again, even though I knew he wanted me to.

Jimmy's Disappeared

We've haven't even been back at Skilly for one week, but everything's horrible already. Jimmy's disappeared. No one knows where he is. He went out yesterday, but he didn't go to school and he didn't tell anyone where he was going and he hasn't come back. He was out all night. Silas

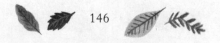

went looking for him, and every time the phone rings, Hortense grabs it and then she looks upset because it's not Jimmy.

Silas and Hortense really like Jimmy. They probably even love him. He helps Silas in the garden and they chat when they're working, and Hortense has known him since he was a little boy. Jimmy really is the old hand at Skilly. Even Mrs. Clanks looks worried. I hope they find him soon. Tea tasted horrible today, like all Hortense's worry had got into it.

Zac said, "Where would he go at night?" but I don't know the answer. It makes me afraid to think of Jimmy out all night. I wonder if he slept on the pavement or if he just walked around. I hope he's got some money so he can phone Silas if he needs help.

Zac thinks he's been kidnapped, but I don't think so— he hasn't got anyone to pay money to get him back, so he's not worth kidnapping. People only kidnap rich kids. Otherwise it's not worth it.

Jimmy's Back!

Jimmy's back, but he isn't happy to be here. He's angry. He's got dark lines under his eyes, so I don't think he's had any sleep. Silas brought him back when we were having

breakfast. Hortense said not to ask Jimmy anything so when he came in everyone just said "hi" like he hadn't been away at all. Except for Hortense. She put her arm around him. Usually Jimmy loves food, but he didn't eat anything. He didn't even pick up his knife and fork. He's got a wall up in front of him now, like Pip.

I don't think he'll stay for long. I think he's just pretending to be here. I think he's gone already.

Back to School

We went back to school today. It felt funny writing *1990* in my book. Miss Campbell got us to think about new things that might be invented in the 1990s.

One girl said everyone will be able to talk to each other through computers. Her dad told her about it. She said people won't have to work in offices anymore. They can just stay at home and work. They could even stay in their pajamas and no one would know. They'd still have to get dressed to go shopping though.

One boy said there'll be backpacks with engines, and if you pull a string, you'll be able to fly. Kaleigh said maybe everyone would be able to change the way they look just by eating a pill. I said I think we might live on the moon because it's getting too crowded down here.

Pip doesn't normally say anything, but she said maybe there'd be special helmets and if we put them on and shut our eyes we could go anywhere we imagined, even back to the past. It was the best idea of all.

More Photos of a Dog

Martha sent us some photos. They came today! There's one of me in the garden with Dash, one of Zac throwing a stick to Dash and one of us all on the sofa on New Year's Day. Me and Zac are sitting on each side and Dash is in the middle. Martha's not in it because she took the photo.

Hortense said why don't we put the one with all of us in our Memory Book, so we did. We glued it in really carefully, and I wrote *Dash, New Year 1990*. I tried to write neatly like Glenda, but I couldn't. All the letters went in different directions.

Then Zac said, "Can I look at the other photo of the dog?" So we looked at the photo from when we were babies. Then we looked at the other pages, and the memories seemed such a long time ago and so far away. I felt quite sad.

Hortense said, "That was then and this is now, and now's okay isn't it?" And she smiled, and me and Zac nodded. Because it is.

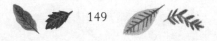

Snow

It snowed all night, and now it feels like the world's stopped turning, like nothing's moving anymore. Everything's white and soft and the garden looks beautiful, and all the cars are stuck so if you want to go anywhere you have to walk.

Hortense and Silas took us sledding in the park. Everyone went except Mrs. Clanks. Even Jimmy. Esther wanted to wear her yellow shoes, but she put on wellie boots because she wasn't allowed to come if she didn't. There's a cupboard full of wellies, and someone would have to have really enormous feet like Silas's or tiny feet like a baby's for there not to be some that fit. There weren't any yellow ones though. She had to wear green.

Pip came too. She didn't mind what she wore as long as she had her jumper. She wore her Christmas jumper underneath, and Zac gave her his earmuffs, and Hortense put a coat on top and wrapped her in a scarf and put a hat on her head. You could hardly tell who she was. She looked like a bundle of clothes. When we were walking to the park I put my arm through hers, and she didn't mind. It was really cold, and our breath was like smoke, and it felt so nice.

We went to the park early because people go crazy on sleds there. You could get killed even, because they go so fast. People make sleds out of anything. They use bits of metal and big wooden doors and canoes. Last year a girl went down on an office chair with wheels on. She was spinning around and screaming, but she didn't fall off until she got to the bottom. Then she climbed back up the hill but left the chair, and people did all sorts of things with it, and when the snow melted it was still there for weeks afterward. But I don't think you could use it as an office chair anymore. It was falling apart.

Because we went early there was only a man with a little girl on a sled and some people on trays and some teenagers on skateboards and us.

We only had four sleds, so we had to take turns. I went down with Pip. I sat behind her, and she leaned back and looked at the sky and she had a big smile on her face. And for that minute I don't think she was even thinking about her sister. I think the sky was just filling her head. I held her hand when we walked back up. I had to pull her, but I didn't mind. Every time I looked at her, she was smiling.

Sophia and Miles went down together. Sophia was steering, and they went really fast and screamed all the way down.

When Esther went down with Hortense, I thought Esther would be thrown into the air because they were almost flying, but Hortense held her all the way down. Then they lost the string and were about to hit the tree, so Hortense pulled her off the sled and they rolled through the snow. There was so much snow stuck to their coats, you couldn't even see Esther's was yellow.

When Milap and Harit went down, Milap kept his heels on the ground the whole way so they couldn't go too fast. He didn't want to risk losing his brother because he's already lost his mum and dad. It didn't look any fun.

Then Harit went down with Zac, and neither of them put their feet down. They just went as fast as they could, and everyone had to jump out of the way. When they stopped they were laughing so much they couldn't stand up.

Jimmy found a tray someone left behind. He didn't want to share. First he went down facing forward, then he went down backward so he couldn't see what was happening. Then he went down standing up. Everyone had to watch out in case he hit them because he didn't care. He was smiling a great big smile, but he didn't look exactly happy. He looked a bit mad.

Then Esther got cold and wanted to go back, and Zac said he couldn't feel his fingers so he wanted to go too.

Harit just kept going up and down and up and down with anyone who wanted a go, but he never makes a fuss so he just came.

Jimmy had one last go standing up, but this time he crashed into the man with the little girl. They weren't hurt, but the little girl got frightened and started to cry. Jimmy swore at the man even though it wasn't the man's fault, it was Jimmy's. Silas had to run down and check they were okay and apologize, and Hortense said we had to go NOW.

On the way back Pip's boot came off and her sock got wet, so Silas put her on his shoulders so she was up in the sky. As we walked the snow crunched under our feet, and Silas kept pretending to slip and Esther was dancing around and Pip was laughing. It was so lovely.

When we got back to Skilly, I saw Glenda playing in the garden. She was picking up handfuls of snow and throwing them into the air. When she saw me she waved.

Dressing Up

Pip's social worker came today. She's called Sharon. She ties her hair up with a scarf, and she always wears a woolly jacket and brown shoes or wellies. When she was waiting for Pip, she was standing really still with a smile on her

face, like she was on top of a hill looking at a beautiful view.

She took Pip to meet a family, and when they came back Pip was all muddled up. She was sort of smiling, sort of sad. She didn't say anything about the family, but she told me about the games she used to play with Alice when she was younger. They especially liked dressing up, and I said, "Do you want to dress up now?" and she said, "Yes." So we got all the funny clothes we could find and some things from Hortense, like tinfoil and sticks and swords, and we dressed up as soldiers and had a big fight. We raced around screaming and shouting.

Everyone joined in except for Jimmy—even Sophia and Miles, and they're teenagers. Esther put on a fairy dress and pretended she was a princess. In the end I had to rescue her because Zac wouldn't. But it was still really fun.

The Worst Month Ever
February 1990

February is the worst month of all. Christmas feels like ages ago, and Easter's so far away I can't believe it will ever come. Jimmy's angry all the time, and Hortense has a cold, and Zac got into a fight at school, and now he can't go out to recess for two weeks. He has to stay in his classroom.

Me and Zac are going to Martha's for Easter. Martha sent a letter to Mrs. Clanks, so now it's official. We're going for the whole holiday. I've drawn a calendar with the dates on, and every day we tick off another one.

155

Zac's got a little notebook, and he's making up tricks for Dash. He's going to make her an obstacle course in the garden and teach her to go over jumps and through tunnels. I'm going to do a painting of her when she's sleeping as long as she's not on my lap.

Jimmy's Not Coming Back

Jimmy's not coming back. He's been missing for four days, and now he's not coming back to Skilly at all. Silas has been looking for him every day. Then the police came last night, and this morning Mrs. Clanks said, "Jimmy's not coming back."

Zac said, "Is he dead?" and Mrs. Clanks said, "No. I can't say any more except that he will be moving to a new home." She didn't make it sound good. I don't think someone nice wants to adopt him. I think he's in trouble.

I asked Silas what happened, but all he said was Jimmy's okay. But he couldn't smile, so Jimmy's not very okay.

Hortense and Silas had to take the stuff out of Jimmy's room and put it in boxes. Usually they laugh when they do things together, but they weren't laughing at all. At tea Hortense looked like she was crying. She said she'd been peeling onions, but we didn't have onions for tea. We had baked potatoes and beans.

Everyone's sad because everyone knows Jimmy's not okay, but nobody's saying it out loud. We know because if he was okay, he wouldn't have run away. He would say at least good-bye.

If I had a placard now, it would say WHAT HAPPENED TO JIMMY? and JIMMY, COME BACK. It would have one message on one side and one on the other, and I would walk around the streets with it, and maybe someone would help or maybe Jimmy would even see it.

But I can't do that because I'm just a kid. I can't do anything. I'm so sad because Jimmy's one of my favorite people and he was the old hand, and now he's gone me and Zac have to be the old hands.

I think Zac was right. Jimmy was kidnapped, only he was kidnapped by aliens who made him into someone different. Zac says he doesn't want to be a teenager because it's even worse than being a child. I hadn't thought of it before, but now I wonder what happens if we grow up and we still haven't got a family. What happens then?

The Poll Tax March
March 1990

Silas is going on a big poll tax march in London. He's taking his placard. He says there'll be thousands of people there. He might even be on TV.

Me and Zac will be at Martha's, but we're going to look on the news in case we see him, because then we can show Martha. I think she'd like him.

Zac's going to teach Dash to count. He's drawn a chart. First he'll show her two sticks and teach her to bark two times, and then he'll go up to ten. He's going to teach her to count to one hundred if he can find enough sticks.

Pip's Gone

Pip's gone! Sharon took her away this afternoon. Sharon was smiling like they were going on a lovely picnic on a beautiful hill, but Pip wasn't smiling. She looked like I felt when my class went on a boat on the Thames, and even though the boat was slow, I felt really sick and dizzy and kept putting my head down. My teacher said it was because of the different movements. And that's how Pip looked. She looked as though she were seasick and she couldn't keep her head up and she just wished everything would stop still.

When I said good-bye I hugged her really tight so the hug would last forever. Everyone hugged her or waved, but we didn't say things like "See you soon" or "See you at Christmas" because probably we'll never see her again, and if we do it'll be because things have gone wrong and she has to come back. We just waved. As she walked to the car, she curled her fingers up, and I knew she was holding Alice's hand because she wouldn't leave without her.

I hope Pip's okay. She was trying not to cry because she doesn't know what's going to happen next, but she managed because she's spent a lot of time trying not to cry. I was trying not to cry too.

When I went to my room, there was a bit of paper pushed under the door. It said:

Dear Ira

Thank you for being my friend. When we went sledding it was really good, wasn't it? And the dressing up too.

Pip x

My favorite kids are all leaving Skilly—Ashani, then Jimmy and now Pip. I haven't even seen Glenda since the snow. Everything's horrible.

Mum

Something happened today. I can't stop thinking about it. It's stuck in my head and it just keeps going around and around.

Zac was watching *Newsround* and I was drawing, and then Zac shouted, "Look, Ira, look! She looks just like you!"

He was pointing at a woman on TV who was holding a No Poll Tax placard. She was standing with other

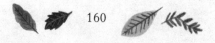

protesters, and she did look just like me and Zac. Her eyes and nose were the same shape as mine and she was angry, and her face was exactly like Zac's when he's angry. She was saying things like "It's not fair," and the protestors were nodding. Then she ran her fingers through her hair, and a curl flopped right in front of her face.

"That's our mum," said Zac.

I shook my head. "She's too young."

The woman said, "We hope as many people as possible will join us at Trafalgar Square for the march. We need to make our voices heard."

Then the reporter said, "This is Bill Jenkins with the poll tax protestors," and the camera moved back, and as it did I saw a dog at the woman's feet. A black dog!

Zac shouted. "Ira, Ira, did you see the dog?"

"Yes."

"That was Mum."

"No, it wasn't."

"It was!"

He pestered me so much I had to walk away, but he grabbed me in the hall.

"That was Mum. That was the dog from the photo."

"No, it wasn't. That dog's dead."

"It isn't! How do you know?"

"I don't know," I said. "But the woman's too young."

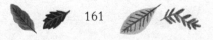

161

"How old do you think she is? How old?"

"I don't know."

"Go on," he said. "Tell me! How old?"

"Twenty-six?"

"Well, you're eleven so that makes her fifteen when she had you. Lots of people have babies when they're fifteen."

I know it's true. Some kids at Skilly, their mums were fifteen when they had them, even fourteen sometimes. And the woman had a black dog. I didn't know what to say, so I shouted, "Don't be an idiot!"

Zac's face went really angry. And now he keeps going on about it. And I can't stop thinking about it too. The woman looked like us and she seemed so nice. She's got a black dog. It might not be the same dog, but she likes black dogs. She wants everyone to go to Trafalgar Square on Saturday, but we'll be at Martha's. Zac says we can't go to Martha's; we have to go and find Mum. He'd even rather do that than see Dash because he says we can see Dash another time.

Zac asked Silas if he could go to the poll tax march and Silas didn't even think about it. He just said, "Nope."

Zac's really upset. He says it might be our only chance to find our mum. I don't know what to think. I wish he hadn't watched the program.

Before I went to bed tonight, I kept looking in the

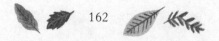

garden for Glenda. I stood at the window for ages, but she wasn't there. I was just about to give up when I saw her running along the top of the tree. She had her arms stretched out like she was on a tightrope. I hoped she'd look up and see me, but she didn't.

Back to Martha's

Zac was trying not to cry on the train to Martha's today. I was too, because the train was taking us miles away from where our mum might be, but it was also taking me to the place I wanted to be most. I didn't know how to think about the two things at the same time. It made me feel sick. Mrs. Clanks asked us what was wrong but we didn't say anything. She'd think we were stupid.

Martha and Dash were waiting for us at the station. Dash isn't tiny anymore. She's bigger and stronger. She jumped up and kept licking us and barking, and then she tripped Zac over, even though Martha had her on a leash. Zac couldn't be sad after that. He just lay there and let Dash climb all over him. He couldn't help smiling.

"I think she remembers you," Martha said.

And now we're back at Appleton House, and I feel really happy again. Martha's got the photo of me and Zac and Dash on her mantelpiece. She's got my painting

on the wall too, and it looks just right with all the other paintings. It reminds me of when we came at New Year's. The garden isn't wintry anymore, and Dash doesn't need a coat. Crocuses are poking through the grass. I'm going to paint them.

Before we went to sleep I said to Zac, "It's okay here, isn't it?" and he said, "Mmm," and his eyes were watery. He's still a bit sad.

The Worst Day of My Life

Today was the worst day of my life. It's the last day of March 1990. I'll never forget that date, because it was even worse than when Mum couldn't look after us anymore, because I was too little to remember that.

After breakfast we walked to the market in Wellsbury. It was sunny, and we were all smiling. Dash was running along beside Zac's ankles, looking up at him all the time like a pony in a circus. When we got to the market, we looked at a stall with shapes dogs can chew. There were mice and balls and little rabbits, but in the end we got Dash a rubber bone. I thought she might be disappointed to have a rubber bone instead of a real one with meat on it, but she liked it. She kept chewing it and dropping it on the ground and then chewing it again. It was covered in spit.

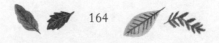

Then we went to the cattle market. A little black calf was poking his nose through his pen. He kept sucking our fingers. He didn't want to let go. Our fingers got really wet and slimy. He was happy too. He didn't know he was going to be sold and eaten. Dash started yapping and Martha had to take her away, so it was just me and Zac and the calf.

I said to Zac, "If I had loads of money, I'd buy him and put him in a field and let him live forever."

And Zac said, "Is he going to die?"

I wished I hadn't said anything.

After that we went to the market square. Three coach buses were parked next to the square, and people were waiting to get on them. They were holding NO POLL TAX placards like Silas's, and they were happy and smiling too.

"Where are they going?" I said.

"London," said Martha. "There's a march on."

Zac stared at the coaches.

"Can we go?" he said.

Martha laughed.

"No, Zac. When you're older you can do that sort of thing, but I can't take you. Anyway, you don't have to pay the poll tax. Come on."

She hardly even looked at the coaches. She just walked

over to a fruit stall. Zac's face looked like it was melting. I couldn't even look at him.

The stall was covered with grapes. There were green grapes on one side and black grapes on the other. The woman serving said, "Very tasty, best this year," and she let us try them.

Zac said, "They're all horrible," and spat his on the ground.

Martha didn't say anything, but I could tell she was annoyed. She smiled at the woman and rolled her eyes like Hortense does. She didn't know Zac was feeling so bad. Then she bought one bag of green grapes and one bag of black.

After that we walked around. I kept thinking we'd lost Zac and Dash, but then we heard Dash bark, and when I crouched down I could see Zac looking for her slobbery bone.

Then Martha stopped at a stall selling brushes and paints and chalks. Martha picked up a paintbrush that had all the ends splayed out like a fan, instead of making a point like most do.

"This would be good for you, Ira," she said. "Give you more freedom."

What she meant was I wouldn't be able to do little details with it; I'd have to stop being so careful. She says

sometimes things look nice by "happy accident," which means you do something by mistake and it works.

She bought the brush and held it out to me like it was a present. It wasn't even my birthday. I was so happy.

After that we lost Zac and Dash, and when I bent down and looked between everyone's feet, I still couldn't see them. We called them but Dash didn't bark, so I knew she couldn't hear us.

Then I saw two of the coaches had gone and I had an awful feeling. I was thinking, He wouldn't be such an idiot, he wouldn't be such an idiot, but another voice in my head was saying, Yes, he would.

I left Martha and ran to the last coach. An old man was waiting to get on. He was wearing a straw hat with No Poll Tax written on it, and he was carrying a bag of apples. He smiled at me.

"I'm afraid your brother got on the other coach," he said.

I must have looked surprised because then he said, "The little boy who looks just like you. Wasn't that your brother?"

My heart was flapping like it was a bird trapped in a cage. It was banging its wings on the bars, and it was really hurting.

"Did he have a dog?" I said.

167

"Oh yes."

The man was happy.

"A little dog called Dash. Is that the one? He got on with his grandma," he said. "I'm terribly sorry you've missed him."

I tried to smile. I didn't want to spoil his day. Then I ran back to Martha.

The only way I could talk without crying or losing my voice was to pretend I was a social worker. Social workers are good at giving bad news. They do it all the time.

I made my face like a mask and I said, "Zac got on one of the coaches that's gone. He's on his way to London."

All the blood ran out of Martha's face. Even her cheeks went white, and they're usually pink. She took a deep breath like she was counting to ten.

Then she said, "What do you mean?"

Her heart was pounding too.

"We saw a woman on the news," I said. "She was going on the march in Trafalgar Square. Zac thinks she's our mum. I think he's gone to find her."

Martha shook her head like she had a fly whizzing round her ear. But there was no fly.

Then she said, "Surely he wouldn't do that?"

I nodded. "The man over there saw him get on."

"And taken Dash?"

I nodded again.

Martha counted to ten again.

Then she said, "Let's not panic."

Her voice was trembling like she had a bird inside too, but hers was stuck in her throat.

"I should call the police," she said.

When she said that, I wasn't a social worker any more. I was a care kid, and I was crying.

"Please don't! We'll be in so much trouble. Mrs. Clanks will never let us come again. Can't we just go and get him?"

Martha looked shocked. Then she touched my cheek really softly.

"Okay," she said. "We'll assume the best. If we can get on that coach, we'll go ourselves. He's probably not far ahead."

There were lots of seats on the coach. Most people had gone on the first two. The old man with the apples was sitting at the back with some other old people. He waved at me and I waved back. I wondered if he thought Martha was our other grandma, and I wondered who the first grandma was, though I expect she was just some old lady. People always try to make sense of things the easy way so they don't have to worry about what's going on.

I sat next to the window, and Martha sat next to me. I

was still holding the paintbrush, but I was embarrassed because we weren't happy anymore and Martha wouldn't have given me a present if she'd known what was going to happen. I pushed it up my sleeve so I wouldn't have to look at it. Then I leaned on Martha's shoulder. She smiled, but she looked worried.

I suddenly felt really old, like my life would never be simple and I was tired of it already. I didn't even know what to wish for. Part of me was wishing we'd find Zac quickly before something terrible happened, and part of me was thinking that we mustn't stop him before he finds our mum. And then I wasn't even sure if I wanted him to find our mum because she hadn't come to find us, so maybe she didn't want to be found.

I wanted to tell Glenda what was happening but I couldn't, because I had to keep Zac in my head in case I lost him, and there wasn't room for two people who weren't really there.

The journey took hours. We ate all the grapes except the squashed ones at the bottom of the bags. They made my teeth feel furry. The coach couldn't go all the way into London because there was so much traffic, so the driver stopped early.

"Where are the other coaches?" Martha said as we got off.

"Not sure, honey," said the driver. "Pandemonium today."

Pandemonium means "chaos." *Honey* means "sweetheart" or "darling." If Zac had been there, he'd have smirked at the driver calling Martha honey, but Zac wasn't there. He was the little space beside me all the time. Missing.

We had to get two trains and one bus to get near Trafalgar Square, and then we had to walk. There was a big crowd of people going to Trafalgar Square, and they were singing and chatting like they were at a carnival or going to a picnic. Some had placards like Silas's, and some had banners with different people holding each end. There was even a baby in a buggy with No Poll Tax written on the back.

At first it was quite nice, but then it got scary because there were so many people. Martha held my hand, and I was glad because everyone was taller than me. You could drown in a crowd like that. You could run out of air and fall down dead and no one would notice. Or you could trip and be trampled to death, and the pigeons would find you when everyone had gone and peck through your pockets for food. I hope somebody took the baby out of the buggy and cuddled it.

There were so many people at Trafalgar Square, I didn't recognize anything. It was like if you spill juice in the summer and wasps crawl over everything until you can't see the juice anymore. I couldn't even see the lions.

Martha put her mouth next to my ear and shouted, "We won't find them here! We need help."

The bird in my chest was fluttering so hard it was hurting. I didn't say a word, but I kept calling in my head.

Zac, where are you? Zac, where are you? Zac! Zac!

And then I heard his voice in my head. He was calling my name over and over.

Ira! Ira! Ira!

I looked up and saw the top of the National Gallery where Anita took us to see the paintings and Zac set off the alarm, and suddenly I just knew where to go.

I pulled Martha's hand and shouted, "That way!" and we pushed through the crowd. I didn't even say sorry or excuse me. I just kept pushing. And all the time Zac was calling my name.

I kept pulling Martha until we came to a lane behind the National Gallery where there weren't so many people. Two women were sitting on the pavement eating sandwiches. When they saw us they smiled, and one said, "We've walked miles." Martha smiled back but I didn't. I just let go of her hand and ran down the lane. I didn't even check she was behind me. I just kept running, and all the time I could hear Zac in my head.

And then I saw him. He was sitting on a step with Dash on his lap.

I shouted, "Zac!"

He looked like a rag doll.

"Zac!"

I ran to his side and knelt beside him, and he lifted his head and looked at me for a moment. Then he looked away. His eyes were all glassy, as though his tears had made a new skin across them. Dash didn't move. Not even a twitch. Blood was coming out of her ears.

Martha came up behind me and crouched down too. She was panting. She touched Zac's cheek like she touched mine at the market.

"It's all right now," she said.

Zac didn't look up.

Then she ran her hand over Dash's face.

"Is Dash okay?" I whispered.

She shook her head. She was gritting her teeth, and the bird in her throat was making her shiver. It took all my strength not to cry. I had to push my feelings right back inside. I kept telling myself, At least Zac's okay, at least Zac's okay.

Martha wrapped her jacket around Dash and picked her up.

Then she said, "Take Zac's hand, Ira, and stay close."

173

She carried Dash like she was a baby, even though it was too late to help her now. Even though she was dead. Me and Zac followed her back down the lane, all our happiness gone forever.

When we got to the end of the lane, everything had changed. It was like someone had thrown a bomb into the crowd. Only the crowd was the bomb, and it was exploding everywhere. People were running and shouting and grabbing their children, and police in yellow jackets were charging into the crowd on their horses and waving sticks, and everyone was angry and upset.

The women who were eating sandwiches had gone. They probably dropped their sandwiches and ran. I expect the pigeons will find them tomorrow. Some people were throwing bottles and bits of wood, and if those didn't get you, the policemen might hit you with a stick. A woman was sitting on the curb with blood running down her face. She was so surprised, she couldn't even cry. She couldn't work out if she was in a dream or real life. I couldn't work it out either.

An old man was telling everyone to calm down, but he was like a leaf blown about in a storm. Nobody was paying any attention. A little girl who was being carried by her mum tried to reach her hair clasp, which had fallen to the ground. It had a ladybird on it with glittery red wings.

I picked it up and gave it to her, and she snatched it and turned away. I didn't mind. I knew she was scared.

But Zac and Martha and I just kept on walking. I wasn't scared at all, because the worst thing that could possibly happen had already happened. Zac had killed Dash. I kept looking at Zac's eyes and wondering if they would be glassy like that for the rest of his life.

It took a long time to get away from Trafalgar Square, but at last we came to a bridge. People were leaning over looking into the Thames or sitting on the pavement staring at the curb. They looked confused, like they'd gone on a long journey and arrived at the wrong place. We could still hear shouting, but it was far away. I looked into the water, all shiny and smooth, and wished we could disappear into it forever.

After we had been walking for ages, Martha stopped a black cab and it took us back to Skilly. Even though one of my dreams was to ride in a black cab, it was the saddest journey of my life. Martha put Dash on her lap and covered her with her jacket but her paw poked out the whole way.

Back to Skilly

It was horrible at Skilly. Silas was already upset about the march, and when we arrived everyone felt even sadder.

It was like we were all sitting in a great big cloud. Zac ran straight up to our room and got under his duvet. He wouldn't come out. He wouldn't eat or speak. He wouldn't even put his pajamas on. Silas took Dash away, I don't know where. I'm trying not to think about it. Hortense made a bed for Martha in Pip's old room. Afterward me and Martha ate in the kitchen with Hortense and Silas.

"It wasn't meant to happen like that," Silas said. "It wasn't meant to happen like that."

He had been right in the middle of the fighting. He was lucky he didn't get hit. He said he was one of the first ones to get to Trafalgar Square, and everyone was singing. And then suddenly, it wasn't all right. He said it was like a storm coming.

"If only I'd known Zac was there, young Ira," he said.

When I went up to bed, Martha gave me a hug. She started to say something but then changed her mind; there's nothing to say. We couldn't even really say good-night because it could never be a good night.

I'd hoped Zac would be asleep when I came upstairs, but he wasn't. When I pulled back the duvet, he looked like a different boy. His face was all screwed up like he'd been beaten up from the inside.

"I just wanted to find Mum," he said. "That was my New Year's resolution. I just wanted to see her for one minute because I can't remember her. I'm sorry."

I wanted to tell him it's all right and it doesn't matter and everything's fine, but I couldn't because it's not true. Nothing will ever be fine again. I wanted to be like Matilda and make Dash jump out of wherever Silas put her and come running up the stairs, but I couldn't. I couldn't do anything.

When I took off my jumper, the paintbrush fell out of my sleeve. The bristles aren't shaped like a fan anymore; they're bent.

I wonder if the little calf's dead yet.

The Day After the Worst Day of My Life
April 1990

Martha's gone. She didn't even say good-bye. Silas drove her and Dash back to Wellsbury this morning when we were asleep. We'll never see them again.

Zac's eyes are still wet and he's got that horrible choking look, only this time I don't think he'll ever get out of it. He'll be stuck there the rest of his life. It's April Fool's Day, but nobody's playing tricks.

Hortense gave us pancakes and honey for breakfast, but they tasted horrible. Honey only tastes nice if you're happy. Otherwise it tastes all wrong.

The other kids were nice, but they didn't really say anything. I think Hortense had told them not to ask questions, like when Jimmy came back that time he went missing. Esther sat next to me at breakfast and snuggled up really close. She knew we were sad.

After breakfast Hortense went to church. She said the world is so ungodly, she needs to say a prayer. I hope she says a prayer for all the people at the march and for Martha and Dash and the kids at Skilly and for Silas. When she left I waved to her from the door and she gave me a little wink. She looked lovely.

Later Mrs. Clanks called me and Zac into her office. I thought this time she'd shout, but I think she was too disappointed to be angry.

"Martha was sorry to hurry away," she said, "but Silas wanted to miss the traffic."

"Can we ring her to say good-bye?" I said. "And say sorry?"

"She's going to ring you later," Mrs. Clanks said. "You can make your apologies then."

Then she said, "What you did yesterday was very wrong and very dangerous. You won't find your mother by searching the streets. Seven million people live in London."

Her face was hard when she said that.

"You will have to wait until you are grown up."

And she smiled her smile that isn't a smile at all. And that's why she has that smile. So she can say terrible things.

When Silas got back he said Martha told him about me finding Zac.

"How did you know where to find him?" he said.

I tried to explain it was like there was an invisible string leading me to him, and I knew that I had to follow it.

"That's your sixth sense," he said. "I told you it'd come in useful."

Normally I would smile, but I couldn't because I was sad all the way through, like a stick of rock nobody put any sugar in.

Then Silas said, "Don't worry, Ira. Give things time."

That's like saying "Time heals." It's what grown-ups say because the one thing they can be sure of is time, because they've had so much of it. It means after time passes you forget things, and then they don't hurt so much. But I don't want to forget. There are too many nice things to remember, and there might not be any more.

I asked Silas why people were fighting at the march.

He said, "Feelings. Too many different feelings all felt too strong. It's always feelings that get things out of

control. If you took the feelings away there wouldn't be any fighting, or anything else good neither."

I don't want to feel anything ever again.

I felt sick waiting for Martha to phone. I didn't know what to do. I tried to write in my diary, but that made me feel even worse. Then I sat in the kitchen with Hortense and just stared and stared at the phone in the hall and waited for it to ring. I wanted to tell Martha how sorry I am and how I wish and wish everything wasn't spoiled.

But when she rang I couldn't say anything. Zac wouldn't come to the phone, so it was just me. My mouth was full and empty all at the same time. A scream was trying to get out but I wouldn't let it, because if it did it might not stop.

At last I said, really quietly so the scream wouldn't escape, "I'm sorry, Martha."

And she said, "I know. Me too."

Then a funny sound came out of me and I was nearly crying, but I stopped myself by pretending to be a receptionist, because receptionists don't cry on the phone. You could never be a receptionist if you cry on the phone.

"Where's Dash?" I said.

"Silas helped me bury her under the willow," Martha said. "When you come back you can take her some flowers."

181

"Will we come back?" I said.

In my head I was sort of screaming, but on the outside my voice was really small and trembling.

"Yes," Martha said.

"Zac too?"

"Of course."

And now I feel like jumping. Not jumping like everything's fine again, but jumping because I'm alive and I want to be alive tomorrow too.

That's what Silas meant by "Give things time."

What Happened to Zac

Zac told me what happened. He said he's never going to talk about it again, so I'd better listen.

When me and Martha were looking at the brushes, he said he and Dash went to look at the coaches. He didn't exactly think he'd get on one; he just wanted to get closer. The first coach set off when Dash dropped her chewy bone, and he was looking for it but then he got in the queue for the second coach, just to see what it felt like to be queuing to go to the march. He stood next to an old woman, and she was stroking Dash and making a fuss of her, so when she got on the coach, Zac got on too and sat next to her. Nobody asked for money or anything.

The woman said, "Don't you want to sit with your mum?" And Zac said, "No, she's got the baby and the baby frightens Dash."

The words just popped out, like someone else had said them.

Then the woman said, "Well, all the better for me then," and she got out a paper bag and said, "Here, have a mint." Dash put her nose in the bag and the woman said, "Bit of an outing for him too," and Zac said, "She's a girl."

The woman talked the whole journey and shared her chicken sandwiches. Zac had the bread and Dash had the chicken. She said, "You're a very little boy to be going to London," and Zac said, "I've been there before."

When they got to London, Zac said, "Thank you very much for the sandwiches," and the woman said, "Lovely to meet you," and Zac and Dash jumped off the coach and ran into the crowd.

Everyone was going to Trafalgar Square, so he just followed them and looked all around for Mum, but he couldn't see her anywhere. The women were all too old or too young or their hair wasn't curly or their faces were wrong.

At Trafalgar Square the crowd was really big and noisy, and people were pushing, and Dash got frightened and

was barking. Zac tried to tell her it was okay, but then the crowd moved like a big wave and Zac nearly fell over, and then Dash wasn't barking anymore. She was lying on the ground and people were standing on her. They didn't even know she was there. He shouted but no one heard.

Then he picked Dash up and carried her away from Trafalgar Square. She was really floppy and blood was coming out of her ears but he kept walking and telling her it was all going to be okay. When he got to a doorway, he sat down and put her on his lap, but she wasn't moving. He kept wishing I would come but he didn't call my name. He didn't make a single sound. And when he realized Dash was dead, he wished he was dead too, and he still does.

Silas

Silas might have to go to prison because he won't pay the poll tax. He didn't even wait for the poll tax people to ask for the money. He just wrote and said he wasn't paying because he thinks it costs too much and it isn't fair. Me and Zac were in the kitchen when he told Hortense.

I said, "Will they send you to jail?"

"It's not likely they'll put me in jail," he said. "There

are a lot of people not paying. The jails aren't big enough for all of them."

Hortense was sitting at the table with her hands around a mug of tea. When Silas went out into the garden, she said, "Bloody man." I was so surprised. I never heard her swear before.

"He just has to go that much further than anyone else, doesn't he?" she said.

"That's because he likes traveling," said Zac.

It was the first time since the march that Hortense smiled. Zac didn't smile though.

Back to Martha's

We came back to Martha's today. At first Zac refused to get off the train. He screwed his eyes shut and wouldn't move. It was like he was stuck to his seat. Mrs. Clanks put her face close to his and said, "I'm not putting up with any nonsense from you, Zac, so get up."

Martha was waiting on the platform. When she saw us she ran toward us with her arms stretched out. She was wearing a blue dress and her head was bobbing, and she was sort of smiling like she didn't know whether to be happy or not, but she thought she should try to be. She looked like a puppet with strings attached to bobbing clouds.

She didn't tell us off. She gave us a hug, and after she said good-bye to Mrs. Clanks, she said, "Come along."

Zac didn't speak all the way from London to Appleton House. He hates himself.

Saying Good-bye to Dash

The house is horrible without Dash. All her doggy things are here. Her basket's next to the kitchen door. It looks like she just got out. The blanket's all crumpled, and you can see a bit of my green dress.

She's buried under a little heap of soil under the willow. Me and Zac picked some daisies and put them in a jar next to the soil, but it's so beautiful when you look up into the tree, she probably doesn't need them. Martha said we were saying good-bye.

Afterward she put her hand on Zac's shoulder.

"You had better forgive yourself," she said, "or I will never forgive myself for not taking better care of you. A lot of things went wrong that day. You weren't to know. No one was to know."

Zac's face was all twisted. He looked like he was drowning. Martha knelt down in front of him like she was saying a prayer.

"Do you understand me, Zac?" she said. "This is

where we let it rest. Sometimes things happen that no one could predict, and sometimes someone gets hurt. You did everything you could to look after Dash, and when she needed you most, you didn't leave her. I trusted you with Dash because you loved her. And I was right to trust you. I would again. It was the world I couldn't trust."

Then Zac began to cry. It was like the water over his eyes was holding back a flood and it burst. Tears poured down his cheeks and dripped onto his shirt. They just kept on coming. He cried all afternoon. He couldn't stop. Then when he had no tears left, he curled up on the sofa and went to sleep.

Now he's sitting by the stream.

The Promise

Martha was nervous at tea today. I thought she was going to tell us this was our last visit. She drank her tea, filled it up again and then drank the next cup all in one go.

Then she said, "I wonder if I could make you two a promise, but I will need a promise in return."

"What sort of promise?" I said.

She took a deep breath.

"My promise is that my home will be your home for as

187

long as I am here," she said, "which I hope will be a very long time indeed. If you would like that, of course."

"In the holidays?" I said.

"Not just the holidays—always."

"Forever?"

"Yes."

"Here?"

"Yes."

"To live here in this house?"

"Yes. You will have to argue over bedrooms."

I could hardly breathe. My head was so full of thoughts, it was hard to remember to breathe too. I was thinking it doesn't matter which room I have, Zac can choose; it doesn't matter if I sleep on the floor or in the garden, even.

"Zac can choose," I said.

"Well, they both overlook the garden," she said.

"To have our own wardrobe?" Zac said.

"One each," said Martha.

"With a sink in the bedroom?" I said.

"Yes."

Martha was smiling now.

"And go to school here?"

"Yes."

"And come home for tea?"

"I think that would be a good idea, don't you? You'll be hungry."

Me and Zac were nodding.

"But I need a promise from you if we're to do this," she said. "I need you to promise that if you come, you'll stay."

Of course we'll stay, I thought. Of course we will.

"Not go running off back to London, chasing dreams," Martha went on. "At least not until you're grown up. I'm too old to run around after you."

"Will we see Silas?" I said.

"Of course," said Martha. "I'm not going to let you lose him. He'll visit or we will."

"And Hortense?"

"And Hortense," she said.

I looked at Zac. He was staring at Martha. His mouth was wobbling.

"Can you promise, Zac?" Martha said. "This is a serious promise."

He didn't move. I crossed all my fingers and wished and wished he would promise. For a moment I thought he wouldn't, that maybe he liked Skilly too much, but then he nodded.

"Yes," he said.

He walked round the table to Martha and put his head on her shoulder. She smiled.

"Ira?" she said.

"Me too," I gulped. "We both promise."

"Right," Martha said. "That's settled then."

It's the most impossible of all my dreams. I can't believe I'm writing about it as if it's real. But it is real! I have to keep telling myself me and Zac have a family! Martha will be our family. We won't be Skilly kids anymore. We'll live in a proper home. Me and Zac can't stop smiling and Martha too.

Zac's asleep now, and I've been looking out of our bedroom window at the stars and the garden and the willow. I keep thinking of that day at Trafalgar Square, and I wonder how the two moments could even happen in the same world. I don't think I'll ever understand.

Things I won't miss about Skilly:
Rules
Scribbles
New kids
Bobbly blankets

Things I will miss about Skilly:
Silas
Hortense

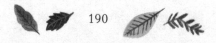

Skilly kids
The tree
The kitchen table
Glenda
Even Mrs. Clanks

In my head I told Glenda what's happened. I didn't tell her about Dash, because I don't want to think about it anymore. I expect she knows anyway. I wonder if she'll come to Appleton House with us. Maybe she won't want to leave Skilly.

Last Week at Skilly
June 1990

We have one week left at Skilly, and then we go to Martha's. It feels so strange. We've got to pack and take down our posters and sort things out at school and say good-bye. Hortense keeps giving me extra hugs. She knows there's not long left, so she has to give me as many as she can.

Silas said, "Just make sure you're happy, Ira."

The other kids look fed up. It's because when me and Zac go there's only going to be Sophia and Miles and Milap and Harit and Esther at Skilly, and that means lots

of new kids will come. And nobody likes it when new kids come. I feel all mixed up happy-sad.

I haven't seen Glenda since we came back from Martha's. I hope she's not annoyed with me for going. I'm worried she might think I don't want to be her friend anymore, but I don't even know if she's here. I haven't seen her anywhere.

Mrs. Clanks

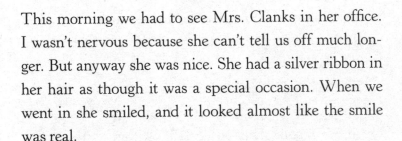

This morning we had to see Mrs. Clanks in her office. I wasn't nervous because she can't tell us off much longer. But anyway she was nice. She had a silver ribbon in her hair as though it was a special occasion. When we went in she smiled, and it looked almost like the smile was real.

"We will be very sorry to see you go," she said, "but it is a wonderful opportunity for you. We will keep in touch, and if ever you want to come back you will always be welcome. If you're not happy, I mean."

Zac shook his head. He knows he'll be happy.

"I expect you won't want to come back," Mrs. Clanks said, "but you are always welcome to visit. We'd like to know how you get on, and of course Silas and Hortense would love to hear from you."

Our Memory Book was on her desk.

"We mustn't forget this," she said. "No doubt you'll have lots of new things to put in it soon."

She put it in a big brown envelope, then she signed her name on a letter.

"Just a few details for Martha," she said.

I was watching her sign the letter and thinking how neat and slanted her writing was when I saw she'd written "Glenda Clanks"! My chest went funny and tight like I couldn't breathe properly. I thought of the girl in the photo with the ribbon sliding down her hair, and I looked at Mrs. Clanks's ribbon, and I had a thought that seemed impossible.

"There," she said. "All done."

I didn't hear anything she said after that. I was just waiting to get out of her office. I didn't even say thank you when she finished. I just ran out. Zac did too. He wanted to play with Harit.

I ran straight up to our room and pulled the letters out from under the floorboard and opened the one from Glenda. Then I just stared at it. The writing was really neat and it sloped up, just like Mrs. Clanks's writing, only hers was more grown-up.

I kept walking from one side of the room to the other holding the letters, like a detective trying to work out who

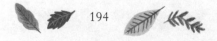

194

did the crime, because I was trying to work out something too. I was trying to work out if Glenda became Mrs. Clanks. But even though I walked across the room a hundred times, I couldn't make sense of it.

I thought of putting the letters back and not saying anything, but then I thought of Silas saying "Seize the moment," so I took the letters and ran downstairs. As I was running, Glenda was suddenly running beside me. It was like she was keeping me going in case I changed my mind. When I got to Mrs. Clanks's door, she sort of pushed me in. I didn't even knock. I just fell into the room.

I think Mrs. Clanks would have told me off if I wasn't leaving.

Instead she said, "Ira, come in."

I was shaking. "I just wondered . . ."

"Yes?"

". . . if you lived at Skilly when you were a child."

Mrs. Clanks nodded. "I did."

I took a deep breath.

"Were you Glenda Hyacinth?" I said.

She nodded again.

I looked at her for ages. I couldn't work it out. She's so different from how I think of Glenda.

"Sit down, Ira," she said.

 195

But I didn't want to sit down. I just stood there holding the letters, trying to understand it all.

"You wrote your name on the windowsill in my bedroom," I said at last.

"That was my bedroom."

"But you're so scary," I said, "and Glenda isn't scary at all. She's my friend."

Mrs. Clanks said, "Am I scary? I don't mean to be."

I nodded.

"You know, Ira," she said, "it's too hard to love all the children who come to Skilly, all the children who come and go. It was too hard when I was a child, and it's too hard now. I'm sure you know that. My job is to try to make things the best I can for you and if possible find a way for you to leave here and go somewhere happier."

"Did you ever get a family?" I said.

"Yes, in the end. I spent eight years here and then I met Mrs. Clanks—my husband's mother. I worked in her shop. She took me in, and then I got to know Albert. He was a boy then, and well, I've been lucky."

And then she smiled, and she didn't look hard at all. She looked strong.

"Have you got any children?" I said.

"No, I decided I wanted to look after children who don't have families."

"Like us?"

She nodded.

Then I said, "I found your letter," and she just stared at me. She was so surprised.

"I'd forgotten," she said.

"I wrote a letter back," I said. "You can have both. I don't want to take them away. Will you keep them at Skilly?"

She nodded.

I gave her the letters and she put them on her desk. I was a bit embarrassed. My pink envelope looked horrible, but she didn't seem to notice. She walked around to me and put her hands on my shoulders and kissed the top of my head. She smelled of ink and paper.

"Now things will get better for you," she said.

As I was leaving the office, I turned around and looked back at her.

"Why do you still wear a ribbon in your hair?" I said.

She thought for a moment.

"Maybe it's the girl in me," she said.

Then she smiled.

When I got out Glenda wasn't in the hall anymore. I thought she'd be waiting for me, but she'd gone. I looked all around but she wasn't there. I wanted to tell her what happened. She's the only one who'd understand. If she'd

waited I could have told her about her future. But she's gone, and I've lost her forever. Because now she's become Mrs. Clanks, and Mrs. Clanks has become Glenda, and I don't think of either of them the same way anymore.

I remember Mrs. Clanks was rude to me when I showed her the photo of Glenda and when she read my story, but now I understand. Because maybe thinking about Glenda makes her sad. Zac's always rude when he's sad.

Leaving Skilly

Today we left Skilly. Anita came to get us. Her hair was the color of cotton candy, and she was wearing pink lipstick and a flowery dress. She might have made the dress out of curtains like in *The Sound of Music* because the flowers were really big. She looked like she should be singing and running over a mountain because she was so happy. Because today was a good day and she didn't have to pretend.

When everyone stood outside Skilly and waved us good-bye, I had to look away. I couldn't watch. They were turning to ghosts right in front of my eyes. I felt a huge sob coming up inside of me. It made my chest hurt. Zac looked away too. His face was moving all over the place like jelly wobbling on a plate. He can't make his mouth flat

anymore. He can't hide his emotions at all. One moment he's sad, then he's worried, then he's happy, then he's sad again.

Mrs. Clanks gave us the envelope with our Memory Book, and Zac held it on his lap for the whole journey. Anita said he could put it down if he wanted, but he wouldn't let go. He just held on to it really tight all the way to Martha's.

Today

Zac and I spent the rest of our childhood at Appleton House, and twenty-five years on we still think of it as home. It was as though there were two child-shaped holes waiting to be filled, and we fitted them perfectly. Martha got another dog, a black-and-white spaniel this time, and we called her Zip. She was just as lively as Dash and soon she was running along beside Zac's ankles, looking at him adoringly. We also discovered that dogs can count, though possibly not to one hundred.

Silas didn't go to jail, and not long after the march the

poll tax was abolished and the posters and sheets came down. We still have our Memory Book and the photo of the dog, but neither Zac nor I have looked for our mother since that afternoon in Trafalgar Square. Perhaps one day we will, but for now we have all the family we need.

Martha has been my inspiration. I have moved back to London and work as an illustrator, but there is nowhere I would rather be than with Martha in her studio. She still paints, and though her hands are less steady, her colors are just as vibrant.

Zac became a teacher and is married with a daughter, Bonita. He has promised to take her to Spain one day. He is the sweetest dad you could imagine, and the kind of teacher who spots the sad, sullen kid at the back of the class and tries to help.

Skilly House has been sold by the council and is due to be demolished so flats can be built. Last week we gathered for a final good-bye. Silas and Hortense were there, as warm and energetic as ever, packing and organizing and piling the table with food. The only difference is, a few years ago they married. Zac and I were so surprised. We had been so wrapped up in our own lives, it never occurred to us that adults had feelings too.

Mrs. Clanks was also there with her husband, Albert. She is much older now, but her back is still straight and she

still wears a ribbon in her hair. At a quiet moment she took me aside and pulled two envelopes out of her bag.

"I thought you might like these," she said.

And there were the letters we had written so many years ago, the pink and the white envelopes as fresh as if they had been written yesterday. I didn't need to read them—I know them by heart—but I carried them with me all afternoon.

There were many past Skilly kids at the gathering, some I knew and most I didn't, but we were all there for the same reason—because Skilly was part of our lives. Amazingly, Jimmy was there, tall and thin and urgent with life. He told me the night he left Skilly, he'd slept under Waterloo Bridge. He'd felt too old to live in a children's home, but he'd had nowhere else to go. On the second night he stole a blanket and got into a fight; on his third night he was moved to a hostel. His life has been tumultuous, but throughout it all he has stayed close to Silas and Hortense. He now works with young people, and he finally feels he is keeping his head above water.

Wonderfully, Pip was there too. I have often worried about the small, sad girl stuck behind her wall, but there she was, smiling and happy with two small daughters of her own and no possibility of a wall because her girls are completely enchanting. If ever there was a small miracle, it was for me the sight of Bonita playing with the two little girls while Zac stood proudly by.

The garden at Skilly was overgrown and bursting with flowers, and clematis and ivy almost covered the walls. The tree had been sliced into pieces and piled high, the names we carved into the bark buried in the heap.

Later Silas lit a fire and we gathered around, a circle of ghosts watching the flickering flames, and I thought of all the lost children who had gazed out on that garden and wondered what the future would bring, or even if there would be a future.

I walked over to Mrs. Clanks and held out the letters. She nodded. There was no need to speak. We took a letter each, crumpled them into balls and tossed them into the flames. They twisted and tumbled a little, and then they caught light, scattering their embers into the fire.

Acknowledgments

I would like to thank my agent, Gillie Russell, for her support and encouragement and for making so much possible. Many thanks also to the wonderful team at Nosy Crow for believing in this book from the start and picking it up and running with it with such enthusiasm. I could not have asked for more. Huge thanks also to Katie Harnett for her beautiful illustrations.

I would also like to thank my friends and family for their support, in particular Paul, Hilary and Kate for their patient encouragement, Phoebe for her excellent advice and Tess for being a breath of fresh air.

Finally, thank you to Rosie and Oliver for being a constant source of inspiration—and distraction—and for putting up with my moods (sorry about the spinach incident). Many thanks also to Duncan for believing in me and my stories, even when things showed no sign of working out.